Drakonian Sa

Dragon of Darkness

Clarence X. Johnson

Illustrations by:

María de los Ángeles Alessandra

ROYAL MEDIA
AND PUBLISHING LLC

Royal Media and Publishing
P. O. Box 4321
Jeffersonville, IN 47131
502-802-5385
http://www.royalmediaandpublishing.com

Cover Design: Bill Lacy

ISBN-13: 978-1-946111-54-8

Printed in the United States of America

Table of Contents

Prologue   v

Chapter 1   1

Chapter 2   13

Chapter 3   29
Fourteen Days Until the Crucible
Chapter 4   43
Thirteen days until the Crucible
Chapter 5   53
Twelve days until the Crucible
Chapter 6   63
Twelve Days until the Crucible
Chapter 7   73

Chapter 8   83
Eleven Days until the Crucible
Chapter 9   109
Ten Days until the Crucible
Chapter 10   129
Three days until the Crucible
Chapter 11   157
Two Days until the Crucible
Chapter 12   185
One day until the Crucible
Chapter 13   197
Day of the Crucible

Prologue

In the beginning, D'Merrion, the king of the gods, decided that man was too arrogant for their own good. He then created different creatures to topple man from their throne of dominion. The other gods didn't take too kindly to this action and banished D'Merrion from their Elyzium to the deepest chambers of the netherworld. The nine remaining gods led the humans in crusades against the creatures D'Merrion created. The creatures who were created by D'Merrion banded together, with all of them combined, they were able to stalemate the humans. But none of them could compare to the power of a god, much less nine of them. The creatures, after being pushed to the brink of desperation, decided to fight a god with one of their own. However, the only god that would stand with them was in the deepest part of the netherworld, a place where no creature or man would go willingly. Having decided that it was their only option, the creatures took a child born from a dragon and a human to sacrifice to the caged god. To them the dragon hybrid was an abomination unto them and unto their god. As they made their way through the deepest parts of the netherworld, they came to what they were looking for. D'Merrion, king of the gods, was trapped in a place where the light feared to go and the darkness dared not touch. The kings prison was void of everything. The creatures built an altar and placed the child on it, desperation flowing through them like water through a river. Stabbing the child through the heart and allowing its blood to flow through the chains that bound the king, something they least expected happened. The child began to cry, showing that it was still alive, the king was in awe. He looked closer and noticed the child's soul was a mix of white and gold. At that moment, the king knew what he needed to do. He demanded the creatures bring him the child. The fallen god began to chant in a language only known to the gods. After finishing his chant, the king spoke. "I see who you are child and I see what you would have become, but now your soul shall be the key to my freedom." The chains around the king began to wither away. "Do not fret, you will have the power of a god, you will be my instrument of destruction, my weapon of annihilation, you will become my dragon of darkness.

Drakonian Saga:

Dragon of Darkness

Chapter 1

Drakonis wore his normal black armor, it was dark and sinister with a white tint to it. The shoulder pads each had four sharp points and with gauntlets that ended with spikes on the knuckles. He stood in front of a human stronghold that sat in the ruins of the once great city of New York. He remembered it was about a decade or so ago when D'Merrion started his siege on the human race. New York was the first one to go as a message to the world that humans were no longer the alpha species. Now he was back to destroy this settlement that was made from its remains. His soldiers ran forth and so did theirs; humans ran up with anything they could find while the smarter ones sat back and shot at his men. His men began to tear through their army. Drakonis' longtime acquaintance and general, Ashnel, began to speak.

"Look at these disgusting humans thinking they could stand against you and Father. It'll be fun to watch them squirm. May I?" he said gesturing towards the battle. Drakonis just nodded. Ashnel ran forward and unstrapped the double-sided scythe on his back and began cutting down the humans. Drakonis watched as his friend enjoyed himself.

'Friend' was an exaggeration; they were barely acquaintances. Ashnel was a lycan from one of the many clans around the world. Drakonis had rescued him from the humans that experimented on him. Ashnel then pledged his loyalty to the king and his loyalty knew no bounds, but he had obvious weaknesses. His pride and arrogance were obvious, and he played for the one with the most power. Ashnel continued to cut down the humans, and then began to deflect the bullets that were being sent his way. He didn't notice the giant bolder flying towards him until he saw a black and red blur rush past him. There, Drakonis stood with the boulder in his hand. He flicked his hand and sent it back to the stronghold. Drakonis looked over at Ashnel.

"You're getting sloppy, don't underestimate them." Ashnel just smiled. Then nine bright lights came from the stronghold and landed not one hundred feet from the duo. It was the Nine Divine Knights, a group of people chosen to fight against D'Merrion and his followers. One of the knights walked forth.

"Drakonis!" He yelled, "I would like to challenge you to a one-on-one duel to decide the fate of this stronghold."

Drakonis stood there with his arms crossed, while Ashnel and the rest of the army began to laugh. Ashnel stepped forward and spoke loudly.

"So, do you think you could defeat Drakonis? You poor boy! It'll take more than guts and valor to conquer this darkness; more than iron and steel to forge a path to survival. It will take a might so great to even scratch the surface of Drakonis' power!" The man rushed forth, pulled out twin swords and started going toe-to-toe with Ashnel.

Drakonis stood and watched the encounter, deciding not to intervene. His normal human eyes turned to dragon-like slits. He looked at each of the divines; and more specifically, he looked at their souls. Everything had a soul and depending on the type of personality they had, then their souls would reflect their color. There were black, red, blue, green, white, gold and many others. White souls could only be found in children, and gold souls were nearly impossible to find. In all his life and travels, he only knew of one person with a gold soul and that was his dad. As he looked at each of their souls, one stuck out to him to be a gold soul but with a hint of darkness which shouldn't be possible. Drakonis was brought out of his daze when he heard something. He brought his sword up to block a shot from one of the divines' weapons. Drakonis turned the sword and cut another bullet into half. He looked back to see one of the knights who was holding a long gun. Faster than anyone could think, Drakonis was in the knight's face. Drakonis grabbed the knight's chest and pulled out its soul to the amazement of the remaining knights. The knight fell over and died. Drakonis looked up and smiled at the rest. Drakonis then swung his sword diagonally at the knights, and at first nothing happened.

Then suddenly, a crimson wave made its way towards them and cut through the air like nothing they've ever seen before tearing the earth right from the ground. As soon as it made impact with where the knights were standing, the area exploded sending debris and knights everywhere.

Ashnel jumped back to where Drakonis stood and whistled, "Wow, I've never seen you use that much power before."

Drakonis looked to where the knights were, and his dragon eyes narrowed. He looked through the dust to see that one of the knights had somehow blocked his attack. A smirk formed at the edge of his lips. He began to move forward, but then he stopped in front of the knight that blocked his attack. The knight tried to pull up his weapon, but it was to no avail. The man fell to his knees. Drakonis reached down, touched the knight's back and pulled out his soul. Drakonis chuckled,

"Two down and seven to go." Three other knights appeared from out of the dust and charged at Drakonis. Each of their weapons were different, and they ranged from guns to swords. Drakonis brought his sword up to block the attacks brought before him. The knights attacked him from all sides, but he defended himself without even moving from his spot. Drakonis was about to retaliate until he turned and saw one of the knights drawing some sort of seal in the air with his sword. It was the one with the golden soul. The three knights that were engaging with him jumped back as multiple gold chains shot from the giant seal. Drakonis watched as the chains made their way towards him at a very fast pace; but all of a sudden, a dragon landed in front of him and took the hit. Normally Drakonis would have been angry, but the dragon didn't move after the hit. Sensing that something was wrong, Drakonis quickly made his way to the dragon. He saw the chains dragging the soul from the dragon and placed it into the seal. The dragon fell down landing at the feet of Drakonis. He could see the dragon's life fading from his closing eyes. Drakonis uttered a word before the sky turned red and the clouds turned black, "Grandfather..." The knights cheered believing that they'd won until that single word was uttered, and the sky turned red as the clouds turned black. They turned to see Drakonis standing looking towards them as his aura screamed power.

"Isobel!" one knight screamed at another. Drakonis then appeared in front of the knight now known as Isobel. He grabbed her by her neck and lifted her off the ground. The rest of the knights charged at him, and he pulled out his dragon scale sword and started to block all of the attacks from the knights. Another knight swung his sword and almost cut Drakonis' arm off had he not released the knight that he held in his hand. The knight grabbed his fallen comrade and tried to run, while the rest of the knights covered them as they retreated. But one by one, Drakonis stole each of their souls. Drakonis' eyes narrowed as the last two knights stood before him, and they weren't going to escape. The knight helping Isobel pulled out his sword and charged at Drakonis with rage filled eyes. Drakonis just watched as the knight charged at him.

"Come, boy, do you feel the power that rage offers you? You feel stronger, and faster." The knight started swinging wildly. "But it has its' weaknesses, you become reckless, and blind to obvious attacks."

He said going on the offensive, "And it'll be the last mistake you'll ever make." Drakonis brought his sword down. The knight tried to block, but his sword broke in half. The knight fell to his knees with Drakonis' sword sticking through his chest.

"Chase!" Isobel screamed. She threw her helmet off and ran up to the fallen knight. Drakonis looked at the knight. Her chestnut hair blew in the wind. She ran and slid down next to Chase and tried to pull the sword out. But as soon as she grabbed the hilt, the hilt started to spike up. She didn't give up. She grabbed the sword with both hands and pulled it out. She placed her bleeding hands on his chest and tried to heal him, but the sword had done something to the knight.

"You brought this upon yourself." Drakonis said, looking at her. Isobel met his gaze, and Drakonis was surprised at her golden eyes.

"Drakonis!" She said, "If I return the dragon's soul, would you do the same for my fallen comrades and allow us to live?" Drakonis looked and thought for a moment.

"You will save my grandfather, and I'll bring your comrades back to life. But in exchange for their restorations, you must swear an allegiance to me." Drakonis relented, and Isobel's eyes widened before she looked over at Chase and her other fallen comrades.

"I accept!" Drakonis cut his own hand and drew a dragon symbol on her neck in his blood. It began to sizzle and became a permanent part of her body. To his surprise, another one appeared on the other side of her neck but it looked beyond menacing. Isobel got up and walked towards the fallen dragon. She drew a type of seal that expanded and covered the dragon's body. Lo and behold, the dragon's soul returned to his body. The giant dragon rose to its feet and looked at the battlefield, then down at the girl in front of him who stood there without fear.

Drakonis walked up to the dragon, "I'm glad you're alright, but you will be punished for pulling that stunt." A smile just tugged at the dragon's lips.

"Yes, young master!" The Dragon turned to Isobel and bowed his head. Isobel turned to Drakonis.

"I kept my end of the bargain, now you hold up yours." Ashnel walked up to Drakonis.

"Drakonis, this is a perfect time to kill her and let the knights stay dead so that no one else can defy Father." Drakonis sat there and thought about it.

Isobel was astounded, she grabbed Drakonis arm, "No, we had a deal. You have to honor that deal." Drakonis turned to her and glared. He was about to say something, but then his grandfather's voice interrupted...

"Drakonis, we as dragons have a high sense of honor, and dishonoring your agreement would bring disrespect to you and your family." Ashnel turned and glared at the dragon.

"Listen here, you overgrown lizard..." Ashnel said angrily, but then instantly shut his mouth when the dragon eyed him furiously.

"Boy, you are far too young to even be considered a speck to me. Do not try to anger me." Ashnel turned away as Drakonis pondered for a moment. He had his men gather each of the knights' bodies and line them up. Drakonis pulled out the souls that were now in the form of orbs, and then placed them inside each of the bodies. The bodies began to heal and each knight got up. It took them a minute to understand their surroundings before getting into a fighting position, but then they realized that they had no weapons.

"What sorcery is this?" The knights saw Isobel standing next to Drakonis.

"Isobel" Chase said, "Why are you standing next to that monster?"

Isobel walked forward and stood in front of her comrades. "In exchange for my life and bringing back the dragon, Drakonis has brought you back and decided to spare you." She answered.

The knights got into a battle stance. Chase stepped forward.

"Isobel, we can't let you do this," he pleaded. Drakonis decided to make his presence known, "You can and you will, or I'll just have her put you back in the ground." Isobel turned and glared daggers at him.

"You can't do that." She protested.

"Oh, on the contrary, that mark not only marks you as mine, but also gives me control over what you do. So if I ordered you to kill them, you'd have no choice but to do so."

Drakonis smirked, then turned towards the knights and said, "Now leave, and I will take your weapons." The knights knowing that they could not do anything began to retreat all at once. Chase stayed and stared at Drakonis.

"Drakonis," he said starting to bow. "My main mission is to protect Lady Isobel. So, I ask that you allow me to accompany you." Isobel watched this as Chase conversed with Drakonis, and she was about to yell no until she was interrupted.

"Very well, I will allow this. But if you attempt to take anyone's life, I'll kill you." Drakonis turned, then stopped and looked back at Chase, "Again."

He looked towards his grandfather and yelled, "Grandfather! As your punishment, you will fly us to the capital. Ashnel you will take the army and destroy this stronghold, then return to the capital." Ashnel fumed, but he knew better than anyone the extent of Drakonis' power.

"Yes sir!" Drakonis walked towards his grandfather and jumped on his back. He ushered Isobel and Chase onto the dragon, and so their fate intertwined.

Chapter 2

As Drakonis sat on his grandfather's back, he began to think of why he had allowed them to live. Was it for his family's honor or was it something about Isobel? No, it was for his grandfather's life. He turned to see Chase holding onto Isobel while she was staring at him.

"Isobel!" Drakonis said looking her dead in the eyes. "What are you?"

"Why should I answer you?" She said with venom in her voice. Drakonis snorted.

"You're a very difficult individual, aren't you?" She started to glare at him.

"Well, I'm sorry that I'm not usually joyful about being forced into servitude." They heard a deep rumbling noise which was coming from the dragon they were riding. He turned his head back and began to speak.

"She's like you in a way; a demigod." Isobel and Chase were surprised.

"Excuse me, Dragon." Isobel said.

"How do you know that?" The dragon continued to fly. "After the dark dragon drove nearly all of the dragons to extinction, your predecessors came in to finish the job. I was a newborn hatchling when the demigods raided our nest during the night, but nobody was ready as they slaughtered us. They were shouting out how they were the sons and daughters of the divines who were to cleanse the world of our evil. My mother had tried to protect me, but she failed. I ran out to try to help her when she fell, but I was swatted away like a fly. One of them had pity on me and told the others to let me live, so they allowed me to." Everything was quiet as the dragon continued to fly.

Isobel's face visibly darkened when she said, "The creature you speak of wouldn't happen to be the black dragon of destruction that appeared all those years ago and almost destroyed everything?"

The dragon nodded remembering the events that caused the decline of the dragons.

"The knights should have killed you when they had a chance. If they did, neither you nor Drakonis would be alive." Chase spat out, before the dragon began to laugh.

"Right if they had killed me, Drakonis wouldn't have been as nice as he is now."

Chase scoffed, "Yea, because he's so kind right now."

The dragon turned its large head back to Chase. "I'm not really his grandfather. It's what his mother called me, because I was like a grandfather to her also. But there are those worse than him. For example, his mother is known as the most ruthless creature you'll ever meet."

"We are outside the walls," Drakonis said interrupting the conversation. Isobel and Chase alighted down from the dragon's back and saw a sight that they had once thought they'd never see. It was the Kingdom where D'Merrion resides. The Kingdom was located in the remains of Washington D.C. Where the Washington monument once stood was a statue of D'Merrion. There was obsidian like walls as far as the eye could see. Outside the walls, there was green outstretched land. It was a mixture of modern and medieval civilization. It was beautiful; not dark and evil as they both thought it would be. The castle stood tall and imposing yet was beautifully decorated to match the city around it. Large windows absorbed the suns light to illuminate the inside. The dragon circled the castle until a pair of gates opened on the side of the castle. The dragon began to descend towards the dragon sized door. As they landed, Drakonis looked around at the different creatures. They just stared at the humans on the dragon's back; word had traveled home fast. He looked back as his grandfather lowered himself to the ground, allowing the two to get off.

"Grandfather, go to the healing ward and get your wounds checked." The dragon just nodded and walked off.

"Isobel! Chase!" Drakonis said getting their attention. "Stay close and follow me. My father probably already knows about you both, and he'll probably just want to kill you." They made their way through the maze of halls that was the castle. There were creatures of every kind glaring at them. Drakonis kept moving knowing that none of these other creatures would ever attempt anything. It was his father he was worried about. They came to a stop outside where two giant doors with two guards at each end stood. He turned towards the two who were following him.

"When we enter, you kneel when I kneel. You don't speak; you just kneel because my father is less merciful than I am." They just nodded. Any one less merciful than him was unheard of; but if he was afraid, then they had to be ready. The doors opened to a throne room. It was filled with different arts that were once very prized possessions in the world. The throne was a large chair in which a man of about seven foot two sat, wearing the most expensive attire that power could buy. They walked to the center of the room and kneeled. The man got up and made his way toward them.

"Drakonis; my son, news of your great exploits has made its way back here. We have heard of how you single handily beat all of the divine knights and took two of them prisoner; how marvelous." He said with an evil smile. He walked toward the three and stood above them. He looked down at Isobel, and reached out gently to stroke her hair. He then forced her to look up at him and noticed her eyes. "*Oh*, Drakonis, you've picked a good one here. I may have to take her off of your hands." Chase started to seethe with anger and was about to get up, until he felt an arm on his shoulder.

He looked to see Drakonis standing.

"Father, her talents would be much more useful in the field slaying her own people than they would be pleasing you." He said with a monotone voice. His father scoffed at the thought, but agreed. He turned to Chase.

"What about him? Are you going to send him to the crucible?" Drakonis stiffened. The crucible was a place where all of their prisoners of war were sent for his father's amusement, and none of them survived.

"No father. I wasn't planning on sending him there."

Then, D'Merrion stood face to face with Drakonis and stared.

"Well, then." he began with a smile. "Good thing I thought of it to send him there, I need more amusement." Drakonis nodded. He pulled the other two up and had them follow him. As they left, they didn't see the smirk that played on D'Merrion's face.

"Drakonis!" Chase said, "What's the crucible?" Drakonis didn't even turn his head to answer; there was somewhere that they needed to go. "The crucible is an arena where any human who refuses to serve my father, must compete in many rounds to win their freedom. Each round they fight an opponent that is impossible to beat. There was only one human to make it to the last round, and my father was furious. So for the final round he had to face Ashnel with no weapons, so you can guess what happened." Anger seethed through the two people behind him, and Isobel reached out and grabbed Drakonis hard. He stopped and stared hard at her.

"If he goes into that ring, then so will I. And if he dies, so will I." Drakonis just sighed, and wondered if they were really worth keeping around while Isobel just stood there.

"Drakonis!" She yelled. "I don't know why you want me alive. But if he dies, I will too." Drakonis just looked at her.

"Have you forgotten that I can control what you do?" Isobel was taken back; she had completely forgotten about it. "But!" Drakonis started walking and beckoned them to follow. "There's something about Chase that I respect, so I may give him a fighting chance." They made their way through the beautiful castle where they came to a huge doorway, and they could hear metal pounding. They continued down the stairs, and they saw these giant creatures that were about six foot seven. They were all charcoal black and very buff creatures. They were all working on different kinds of weapons and armor. They stopped and looked at the three and erupted into cheers.

"Drakonis!" they all started to yell. The tallest stepped forward and everything got quiet.

"Drakonis!" He said in his deep voice.

"King Maj!" Drakonis replied. The giant man went up and hugged Drakonis, "It's been a while Drakonis. What have you brought me this time?" Drakonis turned towards Chase and Isobel. The moment the creatures saw them, they began to freak out and they started yelling hysterically while gathering weapons to fight them. The one known as King Maj turned to Drakonis "Why would you bring these evil creatures here?" Chase and Isobel just looked at each other and then back at the creatures, Chase stepped forward, "You call us evil, yet Drakonis here drove humanity to near extinction killing millions." The creatures all started laughing. King Maj started to speak.

"So is it fair that humanity did that to every other creature on the planet? Is your kind so special that you can't share the planet?"

"We know what we did was wrong, but two wrongs don't make a right." Isobel insisted. King Maj turned towards Isobel and started to ooh. "She's a pretty one." He said turning to Drakonis, "But, what's been started won't end unless one side has given up." He walked up to her and bowed his head. "I'm sorry, where are my manners, I'm King Maj, King of the Majes." All of the other creatures bowed as well. Isobel smiled and returned the bow.

"I am Isobel, one of the divine knights and," she began pointing to Chase. "This is my bodyguard, Chase." Chase nodded his head in respect. Isobel politely stepped forward.

"I have a question, what type of creature are you?"

King Maj puffed his chest out in pride "We are the Majes; distant cousins of the dwarves, but a lot better." Isobel nodded accepting the answer as King Maj turned back to Drakonis "Drakonis, what did you need?" Drakonis closed his hand and then reopened it. To their surprise there was a golden orb in the palm of his hand. King Maj couldn't believe what he saw. There was a golden soul right there before him, Isobel was having a different reaction. How and where could he have possibly gotten a gold soul? King Maj was ecstatic; they could finally complete their project. He turned and hurried towards this device that looked like a giant circle with strange markings. He pulled a lever next to the device, and when the device opened. It showed multiple orbs that could only be soul orbs. Drakonis turned toward Chase.

"What type of sword do you prefer?" Chase eyed him carefully.

"Why does it matter to you? If you fail to remember, you were the one who broke my sword in half!" Drakonis just rolled his eyes. Humans were creatures ruled by their emotions, and that's why they were weak.

"You should have been stronger. Also if you want any chance at beating whoever you have to fight, then tell us what type of sword you prefer!" Demanded Drakonis. Isobel put her hand on Chase's shoulder.

"I sense no ill-will from him, so we have to trust him." "I am proficient in every type of weapon," Chase sighed heavily. "Drakonis, surely you would not trust such a powerful tool in the hands of one so young and full of anger." King Maj began. Drakonis smirked.

"That's exactly my intention." King Maj gave him a worried look.

"Drakonis, has this girl's beauty blinded you into giving her friend one of the most powerful things that I could ever make? What if he turns against us and tries to kill us?" Drakonis just looked at him out of the corner of his eye.

"Then I'd have to kill him; plain and simple." The King just stroked his chin and thought about that.

"I will get it back to you as soon as possible." King Maj watched as Drakonis turned towards the door and left with Isobel and Chase in tow. As they exited, he heard a faint angelic voice call out. "She could be the soother of the chaos in him." King Maj looked up and smiled. As

Drakonis walked out of the forge with Chase and Isobel following behind him, he could hear the faint sounds of their stomachs begging for food. Deciding that food would be good for everyone, he began to make his way towards the kitchen's part of the castle. The delicious smell of food filled the trio's noses and made them hungrier. Drakonis went to one of the cooks and told him to have the trays of food brought to his room. Isobel and Chase were very surprised to see that all the cooks in the kitchen were human. They looked towards one another, then back at the cooks. Drakonis and the cook exchanged a few words before the cook nodded his head and began to make the food that Drakonis ordered. The trio continued their little trek to Drakonis' room; they didn't have words to describe how large the room was. The room itself could hold a family of a dozen and still have room left over. There were two bedrooms, a living room and a dining room. Chase and Isobel began to explore the room. It was full of beautiful bright colors. It was spotless and everything seemed perfect. Drakonis turned and looked at the guests in his room, but it wasn't seconds later that a knock sounded at the door. Drakonis opened the door and allowed the servants to usher in with the food he had ordered not too long ago. Just as quickly as they came, they left after placing the food on the table. Drakonis sat and began to eat, but then looked up and saw Isobel and Chase looking at him with distaste.

"You can sit down and eat. It's not poisoned in any way, shape or form." They still didn't move; Drakonis just raised his eyebrow. "If you both want to stand there and starve go ahead; just means more food for me." Drakonis continued to eat his meal as the other two gave in and sat down to eat. Drakonis had to have the servants bring more food, since Chase and Isobel were going through it.

"Drakonis." Isobel said looking at where he sat from her seat. "If you can control me, why not force me to tell you where the other gods are so that you could find them and kill them?" Drakonis finished his plate and looked at the two knights sitting in front of him.

"Not to give the divines too much credit, but they are clever. Every move they've made up to this point has been flawless. However; if they were in that horrendous thing you called a stronghold, then why would they send their best cards out instead of using them to cover their retreat. Yes, taking you both in could also be a trap, but I'm going to turn the tables on them. Any more, questions?" Chase looked him straight in the eye, and then spoke.

"This war has been going on for decades, so why hasn't you or your father destroyed all of humanity and the divines?" Drakonis got up and walked towards the window and stared at the stars.

"About a decade or so ago, my father; the god, wanted the power he'd given to me as a child back so he could hunt down the divines. However; the power he gave me has fused with me so much that when he tried, I frenzied." He looked to see them both looking at him with dumbfounded looks. He rolled his eyes thinking that humans were so slow sometimes. "Frenzy is something rare amongst dragons, even more rare in hybrids such as me even though I'm the only one. A Frenzy usually activates when the dragon's life is in danger of ending. It calls upon all the powers that are available at the time and uses them in any way, shape or form. Since I have the power of a god, what I did when I frenzied will leave a scar on this planet that will never heal."

"So what did you do?" Isobel asked. Drakonis shook his head.

"It doesn't matter right now, the only thing that matters is the fact that you two need to get out of the broken armor you're in." Isobel and Chase looked down to see that they were still in the same armor that they had fought in this morning. Drakonis walked towards the closet and pulled out a shirt and pants. Isobel gave Drakonis a worried look, Drakonis showed them towards the bathrooms for them to change. Drakonis walked into his room and put his armor on a mannequin and put his sword up on the rack. Drakonis turned to see Chase and Isobel coming out of the bathrooms. He looked at Isobel and saw how truly beautiful she was out of her armor. She looked like a goddess. "Drakonis," Chase said snapping him out of his thoughts. "What are we going to do about our armor?" Drakonis looked at their destroyed armor and laughed a little.

"I could probably have King Maj melt it down and make you both new armor; but for tonight, Isobel can sleep in my bed while you sleep in the guest bedroom." Chase raised his eyebrow at Drakonis.

"And where will you be sleeping? Because despite how things are happening, I trust you about as far as I could throw you." Drakonis just looked at him.

"Considering the fact that you couldn't even pick me up, that says something. But since you asked; I have somewhere else I need to be, but tomorrow we are going to start your training for the crucible. Before you say anything; you have to realize that everyone in that arena is fighting for survival, so they will stab you in the back. Depending on who you have to fight, you'll need all the training you can get." Drakonis left the room and proceeded toward a part of the castle he could sleep in, but he wound up in the garden facing a giant tree. He smiled; this was perfect. He jumped to the highest branch and leaned back, not even bothering with the blue spirits that were surrounding him. Isobel and Chase stood in the room after watching Drakonis exited.

They both looked at each other thinking the same thing.

What have we gotten ourselves into, and how do we get out?

They nodded to each other. They knew that they'd have to make the best of it, if they wanted to survive.

Chapter 3
Fourteen Days Until the Crucible

The next morning, Isobel woke up feeling better than ever but she looked around to see that yesterday's endeavors weren't a dream. She got out of the bed and headed for the living room, where she saw Chase doing some warm ups.

"Are you getting ready for anything that Drakonis has to throw at you?" Chase stopped, looked up and grimaced. Isobel sighed.

"Look! I know this is a bad situation, but let's see where it takes us." Chase nodded, they both turned as they heard the door open. They saw a human servant enter. The servant bowed and handed them clothes.

"Master Drakonis told me to bring you both to him, so I shall wait outside." Isobel and Chase followed the servant throughout the castle. They stopped short when they saw Ashnel ganging up on three little kids. One of them looked like one of the Majes, and the other two were humans. The Maj was standing up to Ashnel, and Ashnel looked pretty mad. So he picked up the Maj and brought his fist back.

Chase rushed forward and grabbed Ashnel's arm before he could hit the kid. Ashnel turned and looked at Chase and Isobel, he smirked.

"I was wondering where you two went. I'm surprised our father hasn't turned the girl into a slave and killed your companion." Chase twisted Ashnel's arm forcing him to let go of the child. Ashnel grabbed his scythe and brought it around to cleave Chase's head off. Chase let go of his arm and jumped back as the kids ran and hid behind Isobel. Ashnel and Chase started to circle each other. They were both aware that Chase had no armor or weapons, so defending himself and the kids would be hard. Ashnel charged at Chase with blinding speed trying to cut him down, but Chase was faster without armor. He began to dodge Ashnel's blows if only by a little. He would get cuts across him here and there, but nothing too fatal. Chase knew he had to get in close to do some damage. He saw his moment when Ashnel brought his scythe down. Chase jumped over it and tried to kick Ashnel in the face, but he was too slow. Ashnel dodged his kick, then grabbed Chase's leg and threw him out the window. He turned to look at the kids, and then back out the window. He made a dash for Isobel and the kids, but it was too late. She had already grabbed the kids and jumped out after Chase. But Ashnel; not liking being ignored, pursued them. Isobel and the kids had landed next to Chase who had glass deep in his back. Isobel helped him up as she looked around and noticed that they were in a beautiful garden. They heard Ashnel yelling as he jumped out of the window to impale whomever he saw first, and that happened to be Isobel. Then to everyone's surprise but hers, she stopped him midair by grabbing the scythe by each side of the blade. Ashnel rotated his leg to try and kick her in the face, but couldn't stop her as she grabbed his leg, brought him toward her and then headbutted him away. Isobel had faltered a little, but got back into her fighting position. To say that Ashnel was angry about getting hit by a human was an understatement, so he decided to stop holding back. He got up and looked around. He saw that his weapon was near the woman and the kids. He turned and picked up a huge tree and threw it at the group in front of him. Isobel got into a stance and punched the tree; shattering it into little pieces, but she didn't see Ashnel appear behind her. Ashnel brought his arm back; he was prepared to kill her with a single punch. He stopped mid swing as he felt the forbidding presence. It actually terrified him, because he knew that it could only be Drakonis. He looked around, but couldn't see him anywhere until he felt the heat of a glare touch the back of his neck. As quickly as the presence came, it went just as fast. When he could finally move again, he turned around to see Drakonis lying in a tree with his eyes set on him. Ashnel came to the horrible realization that he had been there the whole time. He turned and looked at the group in front of him, but they hadn't felt the presence. He knew that he should leave. He picked up his weapon and made his way back into the building. Isobel watched as Ashnel went back inside the building, then turned back to Chase and started to pull the pieces of glass out of his back. He was bleeding, and the kids were looking scared. So she put her hands out to try and heal him, but stopped when someone grabbed her arms. She turned to see Drakonis holding her arms with a serious look on his face.

"I did fail to inform you, that using magic anywhere inside the castle except your room would be a terrible idea on your part." Drakonis walked towards Chase and picked him up; the kids started to jump and laugh at Drakonis. He looked back at Isobel.

"Come on, so we can get him healed before training." Isobel began to follow him until they reached a large tree in the middle of the garden. Drakonis put Chase down at the base of the tree, and watched as these colorful fairy-like creatures began to circle around him. The kids started to jump up and down at the sight of the creatures. Isobel walked up and stood next to Drakonis. She felt so at peace with no cares in the world.

"What is this place?" she asked turning towards Drakonis. He looked at her, then back at the tree, "This is the Garden of Amity, and at the center is the Tree of Life. Those fairy-like creatures were the caretakers of Elyzium. But since they can't get back there, they take care of the garden. They also hold knowledge of everything, but refuse to share unless it's convenient." Isobel had never heard of this tree or the garden.

"Where did it come from?" She wondered aloud.

"Nobody knows, but Father says it just existed; never aging, never having its leaves fall. I come here and sleep all the time; it's the best sleep ever." Isobel just remembered something.

"Drakonis, who are these kids?" Drakonis looked to see that the kids were still playing with the fairies.

"Children!" he yelled, "Come over here and introduce yourselves." The three kids turned and ran towards Drakonis and Isobel. The first child to get there was the boy with both girls behind him. "Hi," he said. "My name is Semaj; the prince of the Majes, and I am seven years old." One of the girls stepped forward.

"Hi, I'm Dior, and I'm human. I am eight years old." The last girl stepped forward.

"Hi, I'm Mahogany, and I am also human and eight years old." Then all three looked at her.

"Who are you?" They asked in unison. Isobel smiled and bowed.

"My name is Isobel, and I am human also." The kids started asking her all sorts of questions, from how old she was to if she was Drakonis' girlfriend, but Drakonis decided to speak up.

"Don't you guys have chores to be doing?" The kids hung their heads and started walking back to the castle after saying see you later to Drakonis and Isobel. One of the fairies came up and kissed Isobel on the nose and spoke softly, so that only she could hear. "The dragon that you seek is closer than you think." Isobel froze if only for a moment. They looked and saw Chase standing up with a confused facial expression. "What just happened?" he said while rubbing the back of his head. Drakonis looked at him.

"To sum it all up, you defended those kids from Ashnel, and you put up a pretty good fight. Then it went downhill when you got thrown out the window causing you to have large pieces of glass stuck in your back leaving you unable to fight, but Isobel began to fight and did a fine job. I then brought you to the Tree of Life where the fairies healed you, and now we are going to start your training; follow me." Isobel looked at Drakonis while helping Chase up.

"Do you expect him to train after what just happened?" Drakonis just laughed. "Do you think that just because he got hurt, he is not supposed to train?" Sorry, it doesn't work like that. Those creatures in the crucible won't be willing to let him take a rest. If it wasn't for me stepping in, Ashnel would have killed him before the Garden would have stopped him. Also; if I know my father, he'll put him up against someone who outclasses Ashnel."

Chase put his hand on Isobel's shoulder and stood up.

"I can handle anything you or your father throw at me."

Drakonis just eyed him. "Let's hope you can; but be warned, this training will hurt." Drakonis took Chase and Isobel into a different building. It looked small from the outside; but on the inside, it was huge with weapons and different items all over the place. Drakonis walked up to a clothing rack and picked up a shirt and some pants, and then he threw them at Chase. "Until I tell you to take these off, keep them on under all of your clothes."

Chase just looked at him. "Why would I wear these?"

Drakonis just gave him a blank look. "Okay! How about this? You don't put it on, and I throw you in the crucible with no weapons or armor." Chase just stood there dumbstruck. "Well then. When you put it like that, I wouldn't mind wearing this for a while." Drakonis just glared at Chase as he began to put the clothes on. Isobel started to giggle watching the two bicker like brothers. Chase finished putting his clothes back on and looked at Drakonis.

"Alright! What now?"

Drakonis snapped his fingers, and Chase fell to his knees. "The encryptions within those clothes add weight to your body. Today it should be about fifty pounds, when you're ready it will increase by itself. You will be wearing it for the next thirty days."

Isobel was the first to respond from the little science session. "Why thirty days?"

Drakonis laughed at Chase's attempts to get up, "Fourteen days from now is when the next crucible will be. And since my father has a divine knight fighting in it, it's going to draw quite a crowd and some of the most fearsome people that I've ever captured will be trying to win their freedom."

Drakonis turned toward Chase, "I want you to do one hundred pushups every hour on the hour, and run one hundred laps around the castle. I will have a servant waiting for you, and they will bring you to where I am." They turned to see the doors burst open and the three children from before came rushing in.

"Drakonis, Drakonis, Drakonis!" they all shouted. They all began to talk at the same time which isn't really nice when you have dragon like hearing.

"Enough!" Drakonis yelled. They all stopped and stood still.

"Alright. Mahogany, you tell me what you have to say."

She stuck her tongue out at the other two kids. "Okay. So after we left you all, we went to King Maj to see what we needed to do today and he told us that he was working on a special project. He sent us to the market to get some stuff. as we were on our way there, we saw Cyarah on that deformed Komodo." Drakonis' eyes widened; thinking that the fact that she's back meant trouble, but Mahogany got his attention.

"But there's more. She had like four Manalourins in chains following behind her!" Drakonis instantly got mad.

"Chase! You do what I told you to do; I am going to visit my father." Drakonis turned to walk out, but then Isobel placed her arm on his shoulder because she could see the anger and hate in his eyes.

"What am I supposed to do?" She asked.

Drakonis thought for a moment. "Why not go with the kids into the market and help them find what they need. But be warned; while you're there, your caretaker will be Semaj. If you do anything wrong then the punishment will be up to him." Drakonis eyes turned from that of a normal human to dragon-like slits "And anything that they put any of those three through will seem like a blessing compared to what I'll do to you." Drakonis made his way out of the door and moved toward his father's throne room.

Semaj looked at Isobel. "Don't worry. If Drakonis trusts you, then I trust you."

Isobel smiled, but then a thought crossed her mind. 'These kids are really close to Drakonis, I wonder why?'

Both Mahogany and Dior grabbed her arms as Semaj led them toward the Market. Isobel stopped for a moment.

She turned back and looked at Chase who was in the middle of a pushup. "Hey, Chase, train your butt off so you can win that crucible!" Chase just smiled and nodded his head. Isobel was dragged out to the market, but she saw how beautiful and busy it was. She was awestruck that there was this city where humans and the creatures that D'Merrion had created coexisted. There were kids playing like there were no troubles in the world, because they were safe inside these walls. Isobel was brought out of her thoughts as Semaj pulled her inside a building; it was a place to buy suits and dresses. The owner of the building knew why they came, because she immediately went and grabbed two dresses and a suit. Semaj put a couple emeralds on the table and they left. As they walked outside, they saw that the crowd was split; walking in the middle were these ten feet tall black mechanical knights with four people in the middle of them who were in chains. Isobel could only guess that they were the Manalourins. She would have loved to help them since nobody deserved to be in bondage, but she knew that if she tried it and got caught, then she'd be putting these kids' lives in danger. Isobel looked at Semaj.

"Semaj, what are those giant things?"

He shrugged his shoulders. "They are machines built by my father to protect the city." Isobel watched as they passed them. She stopped suddenly and got into a battle stance. She felt someone activating magic. Those guards felt it too, because at the moment they also started to gather magic. Isobel grabbed the kids and pulled them into her. She created a magic shield around them as one of the knights got his head blown off. Explosions were happening all around, and the screams of people filled the streets. Isobel turned her head to see a group of people standing next to the Manalourins they had freed them. One of the Manalourins noticed her magic shield and smiled as he started to walk toward them. Isobel kept the shield up as the man put his hands on it. Isobel suddenly felt her mana start draining, and she had to keep putting out more and more just to keep the shield up. The creature started to grin, because the mana he was eating was divine. It was so delicious. It seemed like the girl wasn't going to run out anytime soon, so he could do this all day. He called the other three Manalourins to help him drain her; the more the merrier. They all came over and put their hands on the shield draining Isobel of her mana four times as quickly. Isobel knew that having one to deal with was bad enough, but having three more wasn't going to help her situation. Putting up the shield was tasking enough; but with these creatures, her mana was going down faster than ever and it was starting to show. There were beads of sweat dripping down her face, as she looked down and saw the kids looking directly at her. She smiled at them.

"Everything's going to be alright kids, I promise." They all heard a scream, and they turned to notice that the knights were pulling their bodies back together. They started to attack the group that had previously attacked them. More of them started to appear from nowhere, but the man growled and told the others to retreat. They jumped on the building and started running away. Isobel could have sworn she saw the ring leader look back at her and smirk. The last thing she saw before fading into darkness was one of the knights reaching for her.

Chapter 4
Thirteen days until the Crucible

Drakonis stormed through the castle on his way to his father's throne room. He entered to see his father playing chess with one of the fairies, while Cyarah was making her way out. She stopped when she got face to face with him.

"I've heard that you captured two Divine Knights, would you mind if I experiment on one of them?" Drakonis narrowed his eyes; Cyarah just ignored him.

"Never mind, I shall see them eventually and it should be interesting." With that said, she walked off. Drakonis looked at his father who interrupted him before he could speak.

"That girl Cyarah, she's a particular one and shows great interest in your pets. She asked permission to experiment on them, but I told her they were yours. She said something smart about you always bringing home pets, but I get the feeling that you didn't come here to hear me speak."

Drakonis bowed his head. "Father, your law specifically states that any Manalourin caught will be executed on spot, so why are you allowing not one but four of them into a city filled with the most potent mana users in the world." His Father looked at him, then back to his chess game.

"Are you questioning your father?"

"No father. I just wish to express my concern for this decision, because we already know what they are capable of doing and how they turned against us the first time." His father started to laugh, as he got up from his chair and started walking toward his surrogate son.

"But as a forgiving and just god, I should be able to forgive my subjects because it would be unfair of me not to give them another chance. Besides; after all, I continue to allow you into my good graces after all of the times you've failed. Rejoice my son, because your loyalty to me is beyond words. No father could ask for a better son." Drakonis was having conflicted thoughts. He just sighed knowing that his father was not going to share anymore information with him. He began to walk away until his father spoke.

"You might want check on your pets. They seem to be in danger." He said while chuckling. Drakonis' eyes widened as he turned and ran out of the room using his dragon-like senses to find Chase, since he was the closest.

He ran outside to see Chase lying on the ground with Cyarah standing over him. Drakonis made his way toward him. Cyarah looked up with a smug gaze and started chuckling.

"Your pet is kind of weak. He couldn't even handle Lydia, and then he had the nerve to challenge me in his weakened state." Chase just groaned on the ground.

Suddenly, Drakonis felt something enter his mana field. He turned and swiftly brought his foot down on Cyarah's mutated pet; Komodo dragon. The force of the kick immediately knocked the creature out and put a giant hole in the ground. Cyarah raised an eyebrow at Drakonis' actions. He was obviously irritated, so she knew that bothering him right now wouldn't do her any good. Drakonis went to Chase and slung him over his shoulder. He turned his eyes into dragon slits to find Isobel. He saw her being carried by one of the royal knights with Mahogany, Dior and Semaj on his shoulders. He quickly made his way towards them. When the knight saw Drakonis, he bent down and gave Isobel to him and then helped the children down.

Drakonis just looked at all of them. "Explain what happened as I walk all three of you to your rooms."

...

Drakonis sighed as he sat on the edge of his bed that Isobel was currently sleeping in. The kids had told him that she defended them. He sat completely still, so he could hear Chase's quiet footsteps coming closer. Chase had tried to silently open the door to see if Drakonis was trying to hurt her; but when he opened, Drakonis was gone. Chase felt something touch his shoulder, and he immediately turned around and swung. His fist suddenly made contact with something. It was Drakonis' face; neither one of them moved until Chase felt a searing pain in his hand. It felt like he had tried to break diamonds with a stick. Drakonis looked at him, and then walked over and sat on the couch.

He said to Chase, "I'm assuming you have some questions, so for now I will entertain them. Ask away." Chase eyed him carefully then moved to another part of the room and sat down. He made a thoughtful expression, and he was thinking where to start.

"What happened to Isobel?" It was a fairly simple question.

Drakonis sighed, "They are called Manalourins. And as you can guess from the name, they can absorb mana from anything they touch making them very feared."

Chase was confused. "If these creatures have an ability such as that, then why didn't that monster you call a father not use them in the beginning of the war?"

Drakonis had to chuckle at the words Chase used to describe his father. "Because my father didn't create those creatures, but the woman you fought and lost to did."

Chase went wide eyed and was about to ask another question before Drakonis interrupted him. "Isobel, how long are you going to stand behind the door listening? You shouldn't be moving. So if you're going to listen, at least come out here." Chase turned and saw the door open slowly. Isobel looked tired and weak. She slowly made her way toward the couch, and sat on the other end of the sofa from Drakonis.

Drakonis turned back towards Chase and nodded.

Chase nodded back and continued the questioning. "Who and what is that woman?"

Drakonis just looked up at the ceiling. "Cyarah was once a human probably the same age as you. A decade or so ago, my father finally allowed me to lead his armies. I led the army from Florida and conquered everything from there to Virginia. The original Divine Knights and Cyarah made a stand in Lancaster, Pennsylvania. The battle raged for three days until they finally lost. The knights abandoned her to save their own skins; they left her to fight by herself."

Drakonis started to chuckle. "My father taught me that there were no rules on the battlefield. But those who abandon their comrades don't deserve mercy. So instead of killing her, I brought her to my father who decided that she could join us. She joined without hesitation and founded our science division. She experimented with every type of creature there is. However, after she experimented on me and caused that decade long ceasefire, my father said she was no longer allowed to experiment on any other creature. So she experimented on herself, and the outcome was unexpected to say the least. She has the body of succubus and the lifespan of a dragon, as well as the voice of a siren and the fighting powers of a Valkyrie. All in all, she's a powerful creature. She only has one weakness and that's science."

Drakonis looked Chase in the eye. "You would do well to remember that, because she has taken a liking to you." Chase gulped remembering his confrontation with the dangerous woman earlier.

Isobel thought for a moment and then frowned. "If the Manalourins are her creations, then why were they being chained up and led throughout the city."

Drakonis ran his hand through his hair and started explaining things that he thought were very boring.

"Because the Manalourins turned on us during one of the Divine Knights' raids."

Isobel and Chase both sat forward, because this seemed very interesting to them.

"At one point in time, my father sought Cyarah's help in getting his power back from me. She agreed and attempted to pull the power from me by replacing it with dark mana."

"What's dark mana?" Isobel asked.

"Dark mana is another form of mana that Cyarah invented using means unknown to us. However; unlike mana, it can't be used through a spell or weapon. Dark mana can take the form of anything the user has enough power to create, but it can't be absorbed by Manalourins. Anyway, back to the story. When the Divines attacked the Manalourins, they chose that moment to rebel. And at that moment, I was incapacitated. So, when they tried to steal all of my mana, I frenzied. And when dragons frenzy with their own power, they can level cities. However, at that moment, I had the power of a god due to the dark mana. I am a dragon and a human. But when I reached for something that would help me and felt it in my hand, I pulled and pulled but then nothing happened. When I finally thought that nothing was going to happen, the roof of the building was destroyed and I saw what I had pulled. I'm sure both of you are aware of the Dragon of Darkness that appeared all those years ago." Isobel's face darkened while Chase only nodded.

"I somehow summoned it, and I'm sure you've probably heard; it laid waste to everything. The entire state has been turned into a scar on the world." Drakonis heard a thump. He looked down and saw that Isobel had fallen asleep. Her chestnut hair that went down to her back was all over the place. Drakonis looked at Chase and saw that he was dozing too.

"Chase," he said. "Get some sleep. Because tomorrow your weights will double, and we will be working harder." Chase nodded dumbly and wobbled toward his bed and fell asleep. Drakonis sighed, picked Isobel up bridal style and carried her toward the room she was using. Then he laid her down and turned to walk away until Isobel pulled on his arm. He looked at her and watched as she motioned for him to sit down. "Drakonis," Isobel said in a voice that could soothe even the angriest of monsters, "Why do you serve your father?"

She watched as he raised an eyebrow at her question and said, "For the same reason, you serve your masters."

Isobel tilted her head to the side. "So, you fight for him, because you believe he's good." Drakonis laughed.

"Good, evil, right and wrong are all perspective. It's what you're raised to believe. I serve my father, because I choose to. Because I have those who I want to protect more than anything else, that's why I align myself to him."

Isobel smiled a little. "My mother once told me that good people who are under the control of bad people do bad things. You're not evil. You protect your own; whether dragon, Maj or even human, you protect those that put their lives in your hands. Good night, Drakonis." Isobel laid down and fell asleep as Drakonis left the room. He went and laid down on the sofa and began to fall asleep thinking about what the new day would bring.

Chapter 5
Twelve days until the Crucible

Drakonis woke to the sound of someone banging on door; he sighed as he got up to open it. When he looked down, he saw three of his favorite people. There stood Semaj, Mahogany and Dior holding quite a few trays of what he assumed was food. "And what brings you three munchkins to my humble room at this hour of the night?" The kids started to laugh at him.

"Drakonis," Semaj said patting him on his arm. "You do realize that it's morning, right? Anyway, we made you all some breakfast, now let us in." The kids pushed past him and sat the food down. Drakonis just laughed at the kids, then went toward Chase's door and opened it. He chuckled at the sight. Chase was sprawled across the bed while drooling.

"Chase! Get up and eat breakfast." Chase just grumbled a 'no,' but then he felt himself get thrown out of bed. He looked up to see Drakonis standing by the door with a smirk on his face. "Your bathroom is there. Get washed up and come out here." Drakonis closed Chase's door then went to Isobel's. As soon as he opened it, all three of the children ran and started jumping on her bed. Isobel sat up looking confused.

"Isobel!" They all shouted, "Thank you for yesterday!" Isobel smiled remembering yesterday's event. "Alright kids, let the princess get up and get dressed so she can join us for breakfast." Isobel and Chase came out of their rooms, and saw Drakonis and the kids setting up breakfast at a table that hadn't been there before. As they sat down and began to eat, Mahogany turned to Drakonis and said, "Drakonis, are you going to the annual ball this year?" He just gave her a blank look as he continued to eat his food.

Mahogany started laughing, "See. When he doesn't say anything, it means yes." Drakonis flicked some food at her face, and she looked at him. "I'm not going to entertain your childish antics." She said while pouting. Everyone else just laughed.

Drakonis turned towards Semaj. "So Semaj, figure out who you're going to take?" The room dropped a couple degrees as both Mahogany and Dior looked at Semaj.

"Yea, Semaj." They said in unison, "Who are you going to take?" Semaj started to sweat profusely before getting a smirk on his face.

"So Drakonis, are you taking Isobel to meet your mother?" Semaj had a smug look on his face until he looked at Dior and Mahogany; they had a look of horror on their faces. He turned to Drakonis and saw him staring at him. All traces of him joking around were gone. Semaj looked down and said, "I'm sorry, I didn't mean to." Drakonis just sighed. "It's fine. Just don't bring her up again." Chase and Isobel gave each other worried looks. This breakfast was funny until they brought up Drakonis' mom. Then Isobel chose the time to speak up. "Drakonis, if you're going to be training Chase today, then what can I do?"

"You'll be spending the day in here getting your mana back." Isobel stood up but instantly fell back down into her chair. "See, you're still recovering from having your mana drained, so the kids will stay here with you." After breakfast, Drakonis had a servant come and clean up the room. Drakonis and Chase left for training.

Isobel looked at the kids. "So, why does Drakonis hate his parents?" All the kids looked at each other, then Dior spoke up. "Isobel, we like you a lot because you're really nice and you even saved us when you didn't have to, but Drakonis has done more for us and made us promise not to share that."

Isobel thought for a moment. "I promise that if you do tell me, I will not tell a soul. I promise on my divine power." The kids shared a look then Dior shook her head.

"Drakonis doesn't hate his parents, but it's just that his mom doesn't deserve to be called a mother." Isobel could hear the venom in the voice of the little girl. Something clicked inside Isobel's head.

"What about his dad?"

"His dad died a long time ago. It's better off if I explain it to you," Semaj started. "See, Drakonis' dad was a human named Adel, and his mom was a dragon named Azzaria. This was back when the war was in its beginning stages and D'Merrion was still sealed. Azzaria wasn't as good as she is now, but she led the armies as best she could until one day she came across a small community. She instantly attacked it by burning and killing everything, until a man stood in the middle of everything. He had no weapons or anything on him just his normal clothes. He asked her to spare his town, but she responded with a laughter that sent shivers down his spine. She offered him a deal to serve her or die with the rest of the world."

Isobel chuckled to herself, "Guess I know where he gets his hostage-taking skills."

Dior snorted, but continued. "Over time, after mentally tormenting him with ridiculous tasks, she came to admire and even care for the human. But he on the other hand, did not care for her. She told him one day of her feelings, and he denied them saying that all she knew was destruction and that she was incapable of loving. She told him that if he didn't return her feelings then she'd kill him. He only responded by telling her that he was already dead, because he had been torn from the family and friends he once knew and forced into a life of servitude. Azzaria felt bad for him, because she knew what it felt like to have her family torn from her. So, she allowed him to leave and return home, and he did. When he returned; he wasn't met with the love from family and friends, instead he was treated with hate and malice. He was called a dragon lover and an enemy to the human race. They were going to publicly execute him by a firing squad. However, one of Azzaria's spies who was planted there to watch over him reported the incidence to her. When she got there, he was about to be killed but she saved him. She wanted to destroy and kill every human down there, but she had to save Adel. She took him to get healed. After days of waiting, he was finally healed but his mind was broken; destroyed by the ones he loved. She helped him heal and showed him that she loved him. Over time they had a child, who you may have guessed; is Drakonis. But since children have the purest souls next to divines, it was decided that Drakonis' soul be used to free the fallen one."

"Then how is he alive if he doesn't have a soul?" Isobel asked.

Semaj looked saddened. "The godlike power in him substitutes a soul. So if he dies, he will simply stop existing; he won't go to Elyzium." Isobel nodded absorbing all the information the children were giving her.

"What happened next?" Mahogany scratched her head.

"Well after that, Drakonis' mother started to raise him to be a ruthless weapon of destruction but his dad showed him kindness, compassion and also the difference between right and wrong. Later in life, his dad wanted humans and beasts to be able to live peacefully together so his son wouldn't have to be a weapon. When he went all around the world to teach others, it worked for a little while until he went to what you all called New York. They broadcasted his torture and death throughout the country. To say that Drakonis destroyed them was an understatement; but from then on, his mother hated humans and disliked Drakonis even more." Isobel couldn't imagine what it felt like being hated by one's own mother; it wasn't right or fair. Dior started to tap on Isobel's leg. "Isobel, can you go with Drakonis to the ball?" Isobel was surprised. Then the child continued, "We know you must hate beasts and hate him even more, but he's a really kind-hearted person no matter how it seems. He's even kind to his enemies sometimes. So, we're just asking if you'd go with him."

Isobel sighed. "I don't hate beasts nor do I hate Drakonis, but going to a dance with him isn't something that I would like to happen, and why would I even need to go?"

Semaj beamed excitedly, "It's a gathering of all the great generals from all across the world, but none of them like Drakonis. They hate him as much as his mother does, but he's forced to go since his father enjoys them so much."

Mahogany started to fake cough, "Probably just to torment him."

Isobel scratched the back of her head. "I don't know guys. That's not really something I would enjoy." She heard sniffles and saw that the kids were crying.

"No, please don't cry. I just don't think it's an environment for me." The kids only started to cry harder. "Fine, I'll go. Just stop crying, please."

They all looked at her. "You promise you'll go?"

Isobel smiled, "Yes, I promise."

The three kids stopped crying and started laughing, then began to laugh even harder when they saw her confused face. Mahogany was the first to recover from the laugher.

"You fell for one of the oldest tricks in the book. But don't feel bad, Drakonis falls for it too."

Isobel jumped on the kids, and they began having a tickling fight. She was winning until they started using their numbers against her, and they quickly overpowered her.

After a while, their energy drained away, and they quickly fell asleep one by one. Isobel thought to herself before she fell away into blissful sleep, 'What have I gotten myself into?'

Chapter 6

Drakonis was sitting at the end of the training area to watch Chase square off against one of his soldiers. Since his weight had doubled, he was having a really hard time. A crowd had gathered to watch the fight, and they were obviously cheering against Chase. However, this training wasn't for them. It was to help Chase get better at fighting, because if he lost to Ashnel then the others in the crucible would kill him. Drakonis snapped out of his stupor, as he saw a small needle flying towards Chase. If he didn't notice it, then he deserved to get hit by it. Chase heard the whistling of something flying towards him. So, he tripped the man he was sparring with, then turned and grabbed the needle as it was about to go through his eye. He looked in the distance and saw Cyarah standing on top of one of the buildings. So, he threw it back hoping to catch her off guard, but what he didn't expect was for her to disappear then re-appear behind him with the needle to his neck. Cyarah dragged the needle across his neck and smiled.

"He would be a great one to experiment on." Chase grabbed her arm and twisted it trying to pin her, but he didn't account for her flexibility. She turned her body and wrapped her legs around him. By the time Chase knew what happened, she had him pinned in some kind of position that would allow her to break his arms and legs simultaneously. Drakonis was amused that Chase thought he could pin Cyarah. He heard an ugly laugh and immediately knew who it was; Ashnel.

"You know if father asks me to fight with him in the crucible, then he will die." Drakonis saw Ashnel's smug face then looked back to Chase. "The difference between you and Chase is that Chase has something to fight for, so he will keep fighting until he can't anymore. You on the other hand, only fight for the person with the most power. You can't handle losing and that's why in a fair fight, you'd lose to him." Ashnel growled loud enough for Drakonis to hear. How dare Drakonis, but what could he do? Fighting Drakonis would be suicide, but he could hurt what he cares for. He smiled evilly then turned and walked off with a plan brewing. Drakonis watched as Ashnel turned and walked away. He half expected him to lash out at him. Walking away from a fight was unheard of, so he'd have to watch him closely. He turned back to see Cyarah sitting on Chase trying to stick needles in him; he sighed.

"Cyarah, get off him! Chase, get up! We are going to the next part of your training." Cyarah grumbled about people stealing her experiments but got off anyway. Chase began to walk off. He followed Drakonis to another training room, but this one was different. It looked more innovative than the other training room. Chase barely had time to catch the sword that Drakonis tossed to him. It was wooden, but it had magic runes. Drakonis watched as Chase swung it around trying to get used to it. Drakonis smirked then activated the runes in the weapon immediately making it much heavier. Chase just glared at him.

"What is with you and weights?" Shrugging his shoulders, Drakonis just lifted his sword up towards Chase.

"For the next few hours, you will come at me with the intent to kill. And if you don't, then you'll be dead." Chase's eyes widened as Drakonis came at him with the intent to kill. Hours later, Drakonis looked down at Chase who was on his back trying to catch his breath. He could see why Drakonis was so strong, by the way he trained; he was a monster. For every hit he had gotten on Drakonis, he had taken ten. It was ridiculous and made him feel like a drop of water in an ocean. Chase was snapped out of his stupor when he saw Drakonis reaching his hand out to help him up.

"Come on Chase, let's get you cleaned and get some food in you." Chase got up, dusted himself off and started following Drakonis out of the room.

"Drakonis!" Chase called. Drakonis turned and looked back at Chase. "Why are you helping me? Why take Isobel hostage, when you could have just left all of us dead making your job in finding the divines a lot easier?"

Drakonis just chuckled to himself. "When I was younger, those fairies that guarded the garden told me the future. At one point, she said that one day there'd be a divine that would sacrifice herself for her friends and that I should protect her with my life, because she could help me. At that time as a child, I was lonely. My dad treated me like his child, but my mother treated me like a weapon. So when dad died, I had no one. The fairies have knowledge of the past and future, but rarely share it with anyone. The reason I allowed you to come is because you remind me a lot of my father, but don't take it for granted." Chase nodded understanding the person in front of him may be a monster, but he was a monster who had been forced into that life.

"So, Chase, tell me about you and Isobel."

Chase just started laughing. "There's nothing really special about us. We are both kids, who were born of divines and humans. We were trained from birth to fight you and your armies, but we see how well that turned out." They both chuckled as they made their way to the kitchen. They saw a lot of soldiers sitting together, but something stuck out to Chase. There in the corner of a table was Cyarah sitting and eating by herself. Chase tapped Drakonis on his shoulder and asked, "Hey, why is she sitting alone?"

Drakonis saw that he was pointing to Cyarah. "She's not alone, that lizard that's always with her is there, but it's using active camouflage."

Chase replied by saying, "You know what, I'm going to go talk to her. I will meet you back at the room." Chase grabbed his food and ran towards Cyarah all the while receiving dirty looks from many of the soldiers. But he didn't care, because he was intrigued by this woman. Drakonis just laughed as he went to get his food. He stopped as a servant pulled on his armor and gave him a slip of paper. His father wanted to see him immediately. Drakonis nodded deciding to go see his father first, but he told the servant to have five trays of food sent to his room. Chase went and sat down next Cyarah; he could hear the hissing of the invisible lizard. Cyarah looked up at Chase then back down at what she was reading.

"If you want to get in her good graces, then you might want to give her some of your food." Chase looked around after picking up his food, but he turned forward to see that the lizard was now visible and snatching food from out of his hands. In return for the food, the lizard began to lick his face. Chase started laughing at the lizard's actions.

"So Cyarah, why are you sitting by yourself? Someone as pretty as you, should have a lot of guys coming over here to talk to you." Cyarah looked up at Chase and saw his smile.

"Flattery will get you nowhere with me. And to answer your question; it's because no matter how much beast DNA I put into myself at the end of the day, I'm just a super human and, they all hate humans."

Chase eyed her warily. "So, what's wrong with being human?" Cyarah narrowed her eyes at him.

"Out of all the creatures in the world, humans are by far the worst. They only care about one thing, and if they can get that something out of you. If they don't, then they'll turn their back on you."

Chase was absorbing everything she said. "But isn't it wrong to say that all humans are bad? It's like saying all dragons are cruel creatures, which has been proven wrong by Drakonis." Cyarah let a small smile grace her lips. "That's true, but Drakonis is only twenty-five percent dragon." She saw Chase's confused face and sighed. "Before I experimented on him, he was twenty-five percent dragon from his mother's side and twenty-five percent god because he has D'Merrion's power and fifty percent human. But when I injected him with the dark mana, I over wrote his DNA. So instead of being fifty percent human, it is now twenty-five percent human and another twenty-five percent is just dark mana waiting to be used. Do you get it now?"

Chase scratched the back of his head. "I guess. So, what happens if you take any one of those away?"

Cyarah thought for a moment, "Nothing drastic would happen if you took away the dragon or even the dark mana part of him. However, I'm pretty sure you know what happens if you take away the god power." Chase shook his head, because he actually didn't know.

"Long story short, dragons frenzy if they lose enough power that it may cause them to die. But seeing as though Drakonis had no mana and holds godlike power; when he frenzied, he summonsed a creature like no other, its power was beyond anything I've ever seen... But your divines sacrificed themselves to stop it from destroying everything. If you were to take the human part out, everything else would all compete for dominance and end up destroying everything: earth, Elyzium and even the netherworld, but that's just speculation."

Chase thought to himself for a moment and then said, "So, why does the human part seem so important?"

"It's because human DNA is so adaptive to everything, while others aren't. Pretty much, humans are the base of everything for everything."

Chase nodded understanding what she meant and suddenly came to a realization. "You know," he said gaining her attention. "Despite what everyone may think of you, you're no different from me or Drakonis. You may hate humans, but not all humans are bad. Out of every creature in this room, it was a human who came, sat down with you and started the conversation, but it was great talking to you." Chase got up and walked off. But as

Cyarah watched him go, the scientific part of her brain was trying to process if everything he had said was true. It was a human who had decided to sit with her. Did he have any ulterior motives for talking to her? There were none she could think of. She was snapped out of her stupor when she saw Chase standing in front of her rubbing the back of his head.

"Do you think you could show me were Drakonis' room is?"

Cyarah started to laugh, but got up and walked out with him with her favorite pet behind her.

Chapter 7

Drakonis was making his way toward his dad's throne room. But as he walked up, the guards at the door demanded he take off his helmet and armor. He was kind of irritated, because his armor was one of his defenses. As he walked in, he stopped at the base of the stairs and kneeled. When he stood back up, he was frozen in place and felt all of his mana being taken away.

His father just chuckled. "So what do you think about my new anti-mana room? It starts at the door and stops right at the base of the steps." His father stood up and walked toward him with a sword in hand. Drakonis heard the whistling sound of the sword before he felt it cut up his face. He even felt the blade cut across his eye, but he did not make a sound.

"So my son, I've been hearing rumors about you training that human to fight in the crucible, is that correct?" Drakonis nodded.

"Yes father, it's true." He felt the sword go through his body grazing his lung. He gritted his teeth from the pain and said, "Who would want to watch a one-sided fight?"

He felt the sword cut across his chest; his father sneered. "I would want to see it. It's for my amusement." His father put the sword through his chest again, but didn't take it out. "Drakonis, I forbid you to continue training this human, and if you do the consequences will be worse than this. Now leave and keep the sword in there until you get to your room. Then I want it cleaned and sent back to me." Drakonis was finally able to move. His mana wasn't completely back, but he wasn't going to show weakness. So he bowed again, got up and walked out. He was trying to get back to his room; but since his dark and dragon mana had gone, he was pretty much just a human. Drakonis made it to his room and cursed his luck. Cyarah's pet Komodo had smelt his blood and was watching him. Drakonis unlocked the door and saw all of them sitting down talking. The three kids were the first to notice his arrival. They all started running towards him then stopped; looking horrified.

"Drakonis?" Semaj said while turning green "Why is there a sword sticking out of your body?" Drakonis thought for a moment, 'A little bit of his mana was back and that was enough.' He gently tapped all three of the children on their forehead causing them to all collapse into sleep.

Drakonis made his way toward his room, but he didn't even make it past the sofa before he fell to his knees. Isobel got up and ran toward Drakonis. Chase started to get up, but then he felt someone grab his arm. He looked down to see Cyarah shaking her head. She motioned for the chair telling him to sit down. He looked back at Isobel then sat down. Isobel crouched in front of Drakonis, but then stopped. Drakonis looked different. He looked smaller, more fragile and more human. Drakonis grabbed the sword and started to pull it out, but he couldn't. He growled as he felt so weak. He felt almost human. He wasn't going to be able to take the sword out and would probably faint. He felt his arm lift up, and he looked to his left and saw Isobel helping him up. She had helped him to his room and laid him down on the bed. She grabbed the sword and then looked at him; he nodded that he was ready. She pulled as hard as she could and yanked the sword out of his chest. She had most of her mana back from the day of resting, so she put her hand over the hole in his chest and started to heal him.

"So," she said while healing him, "What happened to you?"

Drakonis turned and looked at her. "My father and his new anti-magic are room are what happened. He was angry that I was training Chase to fight in the crucible."

Isobel scoffed. "And yet you serve him? That's real smart of him to hurt his best general."

Drakonis let out a pained laugh. "His best general? No! His most powerful. Probably. He has other generals; like my mother, who follow his orders without hesitation." Isobel just sighed and started to heal his eye.

"Isobel, I want to thank you. You could have actually killed me just now."

Isobel thought for a moment. She knew that she could have, and she should have but she couldn't bring herself to do it. She was brought out her thoughts when Drakonis put his hand on her arm.

"I know I am probably going to regret this, but I'm in your debt." Isobel smiled at him then a light bulb clicked in her head.

"If you're in my debt, then I want you to do one thing and one thing only."

Drakonis narrowed his eyes at her. Whatever it was that she wanted, it seemed it would not bode well for him.

Isobel was grinning. "To repay your debt, you have to take me to that dance thing the kids are going to." Drakonis ran his hand through his hair. Of all of the things she could have asked him, why that?

"And please tell me why do you want to go to that?" He asked.

Isobel laughed. "Well, because three kids who have wormed their way into my heart made me promise to go with you."

Drakonis groaned. Of course, it would be the kids.

"They played the, 'I'm going to cry and make you promise to do what I want you to do card.'"

Isobel turned away knowing she had been figured out. "Well, at least you know why I've been forced into it. So to make this easy on the both of us, just say yes." She looked at Drakonis. He looked so vulnerable; it was actually sad. The strongest being in existence was as weak as a newborn child.

"Fine, I'll go to the dance with you. But be warned. There will be those who will belittle you for being who you are; especially my mother. I know that the kids probably informed you about how ruthless my mother is, and she will be there so be prepared."

Isobel nodded as Drakonis sat up. "Where do you think you're going?" Isobel said pushing Drakonis back down. He glared at her, but she met him with her own glare. "Fine, tell Chase and Cyarah to come here." Isobel got up and walked toward the door. She looked out to see Cyarah and Chase putting the three kids on the sofa.

"Hey Cyarah and Chase, Drakonis calls." They both walked into his room, and saw him lying down on the bed.

"Cyarah!" Drakonis said sitting up, "I need you to do me a favor. I need you to train Chase for the crucible." Cyarah raised an eyebrow. "Why would I do such a thing?"

Drakonis chuckled. "Well for one. I know it was you who probably came up with the idea of the no-mana zone, but that doesn't matter. If you agree to train Chase, then I will get you a vial of dragon's blood." Cyarah's eyes lit up at the thought of what she could do with dragon's blood.

"However," Drakonis continued, "You are not and I repeat, not allowed to clone or make a new dragon."

Cyarah's smile went down a little. But she didn't need to clone or recreate them, she just needed their blood. Cyarah turned towards Chase "For the next few days, the training I'm going to put you through will break you." Chase started to sweat profusely. He already knew that Cyarah was a psychopath, but it terrified him to think of what kind of training she'd put him through. Drakonis gained everyone's attention. "I'll keep the kids here overnight and send them back to King Maj in the morning, but for now everyone head to bed." Cyarah and Chase nodded and left the room, while Isobel stood by the door and watched them go. Isobel turned and saw Cyarah whisper a few short words to Chase which made him turn pale. Isobel then left back to her own room.

Chase closed the door and walked back to Isobel. "Well, I'm going to bed. I hope that the training tomorrow won't kill me; goodnight you two." Isobel watched him retreat back into his room and close the door. Then she turned and saw Drakonis trying to sit up. She quickly ran toward him and pushed him back down.

"Now, where do you think you're going?"

He looked back up at her. "I am trying to go to the living room, so that you can sleep in here." Isobel shook her head and poked him in the forehead.

"No, no, and no. You are going to stay in here, and I will sleep on the couch with the kids. And if I hear another word about it, then you'll regret it." Isobel left the room, and Drakonis had to laugh at what he'd gotten himself into; he began to feel tired and thought, "That sneaky woman put a sleeping spell on me." Those were his final thoughts before he drifted off into oblivion. Isobel smiled to herself, because she'd gotten one over on the big, bad Drakonis. She walked toward the couch and saw all the kids sleeping. She had to smile. Here were the future generations all sleeping together without a care in the world. She walked to another couch and laid down wallowed in her thoughts. She was taught that Drakonis and his father and all beasts were evil, and that she had to fight and destroy them all for the sake of the world. But all that she had been taught was being defied by the kids that weren't ten feet from her. Isobel sat up and started looking around. She felt a short burst of mana as she turned towards the window, and saw a figure sitting on the ledge. She got up and stayed battle ready making her way toward the door to the balcony. She opened the door, and what she saw shocked her. It was one of the Manalourins from the other day; more specifically, it was the one who had first started to drain her mana. He smiled a toothy grin at her and stood in front of her, then bowed.

"My name is Ariel, the king of the Manalourins." Isobel started to laugh. What guy's name was Ariel? It must have been a new thing. When she composed herself, she saw that he was glaring at her knowing why she was laughing. Ariel reached for her hand and tried to kiss it but was met with a knee to the jaw. He stumbled back and chuckled.

"You're feisty. I like that. You'd be a perfect wife for my new kingdom." Isobel got into a fighting stance, but

Ariel waved his hand, "I'm not here to fight. I'm just here visiting my queen. It was nice seeing you." He jumped off the ledge and disappeared. Isobel watched him go. She was kind of disturbed that that freak wanted her. Why couldn't her life be simple? She went back into the room and collapsed on the sofa. Things were getting out of hand and very fast.

Chapter 8
Eleven Days until the Crucible

Everyone woke up to the sounds of screaming. Isobel jumped up into a fighting stance to see Cyarah with a tied-up Chase on her back. She gave Isobel a deer-in-headlights look.

"Why are you staring at me?" Isobel hesitated for a moment. "Wait, why you are stealing Chase in the middle of the night?"

Cyarah looked at her as if she had grown a second head.

"It's morning child, and I have to train this useless creature if I want my dragon's blood, so good day." Cyarah walked out the room with Chase on her back and closed the door. Isobel kind of felt bad for Chase, but she didn't have time to react before the three kids jumped on her asking all sorts of questions that didn't even make sense. Drakonis opened his door to see three very energetic kids, and one demigod Isobel being surrounded by them.

"Semaj, Dior and Mahogany, calm down!" The children immediately stopped everything that they were doing and looked at Drakonis. "Alright now, go back to King Maj and tell him you all spent the night here. But on your way there; tell some servants, that I need a lot more human clothes for a girl and a boy." The three nodded and hugged Isobel and Drakonis before they left. Isobel just looked at Drakonis. He still seemed so fragile, unlike when he's at his full strength. "Hey, Isobel, why don't you get washed up, and I'll bring the clothes to you when you're done." Isobel nodded and went into the room but stopped as Drakonis went and sat on the couch.

"Hey, Drakonis!" She said. "I have to talk to you about something once I get out of the bathroom." Drakonis nodded watching as she closed the door behind her. He thought about what kind of training Cyarah was putting Chase through. He wasn't worried that Chase wouldn't be stronger, he was just worried that he would be too tired to fight. He sat there for about another thirty minutes before he heard a knock at the door. When he opened it, he saw two servants each rolling a cart that had some boxes. He assumed that they were full of clothes. He had them rolled in, and then he dismissed the servants. He began to unload the boxes putting all of the guy clothes in Chase's room. He started to roll the other cart toward Isobel's door and knocked. "Hey Isobel, the clothes are here." He heard her yell from the shower to bring them into the room. He opened the door and started unloading the boxes in her room. When he finished, he turned to see Isobel walking out of the shower wrapped in a towel and drying her hair. He froze at the sight of her; she was a goddess, a beauty that defied all the laws of nature. Isobel turned toward Drakonis and smiled. She stopped drying her hair when she saw that he was actually blushing. He; Drakonis, probably the most powerful being on the planet was actually blushing because he saw her in a towel.

She actually had to laugh. "Thank you for bringing me clothes, but you can leave." Drakonis nodded and left the room still captivated by her beauty. Drakonis went and sat on the couch and began to think about what he was going to do today. He then looked up to see Isobel standing in his face. She was eyeing him and for some reason he felt very uncomfortable. The fact that she gotten into his mana field but his senses didn't go off, made him curious. He couldn't believe what she was actually capable of. Drakonis started walking toward the door with Isobel walking behind him. She was in her own thoughts. She had a smile on her face; but then, she remembered what she had to tell Drakonis. She had to tell him that Ariel, the creep of the week had somehow gotten into the castle and found her room. They came to a stop in front of some large doors. What she saw made her laugh. There were her three favorite little monsters playing on the back of a fully-grown dragon who wasn't even bothered by it. The room itself was huge, since it had to hold a full-grown dragon. There were servants all around him doing random things to make the dragons living arrangements better. "Grandfather!" Drakonis said gaining the dragon's attention. The dragon turned his head and saw Drakonis and Isobel standing in the door. Semaj, Dior and Mahogany started running towards Drakonis and jumped on him screaming, "Dog pile." Drakonis was laughing until he remembered something.

"Hey kids, I forgot that I have something for you." They all stopped and stood there ready for whatever he had.

Drakonis just smiled evilly, "I owe all three of you a beating for tricking Isobel into going to the dance." The children went wide eyed then ran scattering across the room as Drakonis started to chase them. Isobel went and stood next to the dragon. They both stood there and watched as Drakonis chased the kids around.

Isobel turned towards the dragon. "Excuse me Mister. I actually don't know your name." The dragon chuckled. "My name is Xinovioc; but as you already know, Drakonis calls me grandfather and the kids call me gg."

Isobel nodded. "Xinovioc, I have a question. You wouldn't happen to know anything about the Dragon of Darkness would you?" Xinovioc let out a short burst of flame from his nostrils. "That thing doesn't deserve to be called a dragon. No dragon would drive its own kind to near extinction. I swore to myself that if I ever came across it again in my lifetime, I would kill it to avenge my fallen brothers and sisters who died at its hands." Isobel could hear the rage in the dragon's voice. She smiled "Not if I get to it first. The dragons aren't the only ones it has scarred." Xinovioc looked at her with wide eyes. The look in her eyes told him everything he needed to know.

"Xinovioc, I was wondering. Has Drakonis ever loved someone in a romantic way?"

The giant dragon hummed to himself. "I couldn't say if Drakonis has had anything like that before; he was raised as a weapon. I tried to be there for him as his grandfather, but even I could only do so much." The old dragon instantly got a sinister idea. He looked toward Isobel and whispered something in her ear. Isobel went wide eyed and nodded her head while trying to hold in her laugh. Xinovioc turned back toward Drakonis. "Drakonis, come here!" Drakonis turned and started walking toward his grandfather while pulling all three of the little trouble makers behind him.

"Yes, grandfather?" Isobel walked up to Drakonis and kissed him on his check. Drakonis' face turned a dark shade of red. Isobel giggled as Xinovioc and the kids were laughing at Drakonis. Drakonis just stared at everyone in front of him, especially Isobel. He recovered from his shock and just glared at his grandfather and Isobel who thought it was funny to play pranks on him. Drakonis was about to say something when a servant ran up to him.

"Master Drakonis, King Maj has requested your audience in the forgery." Drakonis nodded. "Come, Isobel, King Maj probably has Chase's weapon ready." Drakonis turned toward one of the servants and said, "Be sure to get a vial of my grandfather's blood and have it brought to Cyarah." The servant nodded. Saying their goodbyes, they started to make their way towards the forge. When they got there, they saw Chase and Cyarah waiting for them. Chase looked like he could barely stand. He looked bruised and broken while Cyarah looked completely fine. They all nodded toward each other and walked in. They saw King Maj standing there with a giant grin on his face.

"Hello everyone, welcome to the unveiling of one of my greatest creations; meet Aviance." A little orb flew and hovered next to King Maj. "Aviance may be small, but she can pack a punch with the ability to turn into any weapon the user desires." To prove his point King Maj ordered Aviance to turn into different weapons. Everyone watched in awe at this new weapon that could revolutionize everything. Cyarah decided to speak up.

"King Maj; this defies logic, how were you able to accomplish this?" King Maj proudly held his head up.

"I accomplished this using soul stone since it's almost impossible to break a strong soul unless you're a god or someone who has a stronger soul. It was actually Drakonis' idea; a weapon impossible to break. Aviance has is conscious, but she is a cybernetic and magical being. I've loaded her with almost every type of weapon we've ever forged, and she can even adapt to new weapons. Also she runs on dark mana, so no pesky Manalourin can steal her mana. And you only have to recharge her mana every seventy-two hours." King Maj stroked his beard. "The only drawback is that you have to say the type of weapon you want. And if she can't hear you, she can't do anything. It's a minor side effect, but I'm still working on that. However, she is a great weapon."

Isobel decided to speak up. "Why do you keep calling her a she?" Everyone else nodded, because they were also wondering why. King Maj smiled.

"Because she has a living conscience, based on the golden soul Drakonis acquired for me. She can actually speak and can also learn more than just weapons. As of now, the only person who can use her is me. So, Drakonis and

Chase step forward." Drakonis and Chase looked at each other and then stepped forward. King Maj turned to Aviance, "Aviance scan these two as future users." Aviance floated toward Chase and scanned him, "Future user, Chase, demi god, nice to meet you." Aviance's voice was very soothing and almost angelic. She floated toward Drakonis, "Scanning Drakonis, anomaly, race hybrid, artificial demi god."

Drakonis looked at King Maj. "She's smart, and the encryptions aren't half bad."

King Maj nodded. "Also Chase and Isobel I didn't like your armor, so I took the measurements from them and made you both new armor from soul stone; follow me." Everyone followed him as they walked deeper into the forge. They halted when they saw two Majes putting the final touches on the two sets of armor. There was Isobel's armor, a chest and back plate and arm gauntlets along with extra plates around her abdomen where the chest plate didn't reach. It was a dazzling set with a cunning assembly of overlapping parts with a dim gold color to it. In Drakonis' opinion; it really showed her curves, but he'd keep that to himself. Gaining everyone's attention, King Maj began to speak. "Isobel's armor is somewhat based off of yours; Drakonis, but a more up to date version." He turned and motioned toward Chase's new armor. It was a grayish blue bodysuit that had a chest and back plate. It also had arm plates in key areas like leg plates for his boots. "Chase's armor is a totally new design that I've been thinking of. It's very flexible and made for fast movement." "So," he said rubbing his hands together. "Let's get you both in there." After getting into their new armors, Isobel and Chase were ready to get rolling. King Maj walked up to them and pressed something onto each armor. Collapsible helmets came out from each of their armors. He smiled at his work. "Collapsible helmets. The great thing about them is that since these are both made to fit only each of you; no one else can use them." Isobel and Chase smiled enjoying the new sets of armor. "So, "King Maj said while grinning, "Go test the armor out. I still have more things to do with Aviance."

Drakonis raised his brow. "Don't you think we should try that later since they're just now getting into them?"

Isobel walked past him and smirked. "What's wrong? Afraid that you'll get beat in front of everyone?" Drakonis narrowed his eyes, "I don't think this is something you want to do." Isobel stopped walking, looked back at him and said, "Try me."

King Maj walked up and stood next to Drakonis.

"Drakonis, you've found yourself a feisty one." Drakonis rolled his eyes as they all started walking towards the training ward. When they got there, they decided to split into two groups; Chase versus Cyarah and Isobel versus Drakonis. Chase and Cyarah went to one fighting ring while Drakonis and Isobel went to another. Each of them faced their opponent and charged.

A little while later, Chase was laid out on the ground panting like he was about to die. Cyarah was laying against her pet while Isobel was standing proud; even though, she looked like she had just walked into a hurricane. Drakonis just shook his head. She was a ridiculous fighter when it came to hand to hand combat, and she played dirty. Drakonis went and sat against the wall while trying to catch his breath. Fighting without much of his mana was such a handicap.

Isobel came and sat next to him. "What are you thinking about?" she said, smiling.

Drakonis just laughed. "I was actually thinking about that thing you and those miscreants forced me into." Isobel laughed, "There are some things in life that you never want to do. But if you keep running from them, then they'll always control you."

Drakonis just raised a brow at her. "You must be pretty old to be saying things like that." Isobel glared at him, "Coming from the man who's a couple of decades older than me; I feel young."

Drakonis laughed. "In actuality compared to other dragons, I'm barely an adult." While Drakonis and Isobel were laughing amongst themselves, Chase made his way over toward Cyarah and sat next to her while Lydia started to nuzzle her giant head in his lap.

"So Cyarah, how do you think I will do in the crucible?"

Cyarah looked at Chase with a calculating eye. "It depends on who you fight. If you fought Ashnel, you'd kill him. But since it's a three-round event, father will put you up against people who out class him." Cyarah looked

93

toward Drakonis and Isobel. "However; if father decided to put Drakonis up against you, then you'd be outclassed." Chase was absorbing everything that Cyarah was saying.

"That's why I'm going to train you until you're able to beat him in a fight."

Chase looked at her wide eyed. "Is that even possible?"

Cyarah thought for a moment. "Seeing how Drakonis will have to take it easy since he doesn't want to kill you, it probably has something to do with Isobel."

Chase laughed to himself. "That's because he has feelings for her."

Cyarah gave him a confused look. "How can Drakonis have romantic feelings for her if he's a weapon?" Chase was puzzled. Did she really believe that since he was only raised as a weapon, then he couldn't have feelings for someone?"

"Cyarah, what would you call the feelings he has for Semaj, Mahogany and Dior?"

Cyarah looked back at Drakonis. "That love he has for them is from his childhood, since he was never able to be a child or do anything that a child should have been able to do."

Chase laughed a little; she was possibly right. "So, what are you Cyarah?"

The look she gave him was priceless. "I am a scientist who also specializes in other fields." She said in a matter of fact tone.

"Okay, what are Isobel and me?" Cyarah looked confused, and Chase knew he had her.

"You're both anomalies. Isobel is an anomaly for choosing to save you and your other friends' lives by sacrificing her own. And you're an anomaly because you gave up your second chance at life to follow Isobel; however, your friends are not. They are selfish low lives, who ran and didn't even decide to help either of you." Chase could hear the anger and hatred in her voice.

"Well, you can't blame them," Chase said gaining her attention. "Drakonis told them that if they didn't run, then he'd use the mark he put on Isobel and make her kill all of them."

Cyarah looked between Drakonis and Isobel then back at Chase. "What do you mean?" Chase motioned towards

Isobel. "Ask her yourself."

Cyarah nodded. "Isobel; not to bother you, but I have a quick question. The mark on your neck that Drakonis gave you, may I see it?" Isobel looked a bit confused, but obliged. She moved her hair to one side, and the dragon mark that Drakonis gave her was clear as day. Cyarah burst out laughing as Chase and Isobel looked at her oddly. Drakonis leaned back against the wall and closed his eyes. Minutes later, Cyarah calmed down from her laughing fit.

"Drakonis; you sly dog, you actually made these people believe that you could control her with that mark?" Drakonis just opened one eye and looked around. "I prefer sly reptile."

"So, what does this mark mean, and what does it allow him to do?" Isobel said worriedly. Cyarah had to hold back from laughing. "All he did was mark you as his. Most people wouldn't know what it means but some do, so I wouldn't let people see it."

Drakonis stood up. "She's right. Since word has gotten out about you two, enemies both foreign and domestic will come for the both of you."

Isobel nodded. If Drakonis' mark was to show that she was his, she could only wonder what the other mark given to her by that dragon meant. Chase decided to speak up, "What about Semaj, Mahogany and Dior, since their close to you wouldn't they be more careful than us?"

Drakonis shook his head. "Nobody is stupid enough to mess with them, besides Ashnel."

"Reason is because they're under the protection of the female Majes." Drakonis sighed after seeing the confused faces of the two demi gods. "Have you ever noticed that in the forge there are only males?" They both nodded.

"That's because the females go out and fight while the males make the weapons. Each female Maj can take on about ten creatures from my army all at once and win with minimal injuries." Both Isobel and Chase were impressed.

"If they are so good, then where are they?" Isobel said thinking that if the female Majes were that good, why weren't they guarding the king? "They are with my mother. And the reason is that my mother values power above all else. And since the female Majes are some of the best, she wanted them in her army as her personal guard."

"If they are so strong then, how come we've never heard of them?" It was Cyarah's turn to laugh. "Because Chase, they are good at their job. I know you've heard of the Battle of Moscow." Isobel and Chase both shuddered because they had heard about it, but they didn't know the whole story. "The battle of Moscow was a campaign carried out by the Stealth Brigade which is commanded by Azzaria. It wasn't a battle; it was massacre. Azzaria and her troops went in and left no survivors. She's a ruthless killing machine without any type of mercy. The best of the female Majes are her personal body guards and that includes Semaj's mom." To say Isobel and Chase were surprised was an understatement. They couldn't believe that one of the kids they've come to love had a mother who was that strong.

Chase turned to Drakonis. "If the females are away at war, then what about the kids? I can't imagine Semaj being the only one."

Drakonis nodded. "You are right. There are others born, but the girls are taken to the battlefield to learn how to fight at young age. The males are taken to an undisclosed location to be taught how to forge weapons."

It was Isobel who said something next. "I'm assuming that since Semaj is here, then he's being trained too because he will be the future king. But, that doesn't explain why Mahogany and Dior are here." Everyone looked towards Drakonis. "Dior and Mahogany's parents were killed by Semaj's mom when they were babies, so she decided it would only be fair if she raised them." Drakonis narrowed his eyes toward the door of the building. Seconds later, the three little ones came bursting through the door and that was never a good thing. Before they could all start screaming at once, he put his hands up and they all stopped.

"Alright," he said, looking at all three of them, "Whose turn is it?" Semaj raised his hand. Drakonis nodded as Semaj started to talk. "The king is turning the crucible into a three-day event with a pardon and ton of money for any man or beast that could defeat Chase in the crucible." Everyone in the room went wide eye. Dior pulled out a piece of paper and showed them. There written in black was everything Semaj had said. Drakonis growled, "This has Ashnel written all over it." He turned around to see Cyarah, Chase and Isobel all staring at him, and all he could do was confirm their thoughts. Drakonis was deep in thought. The amount of humans and creatures in the world that would participate was large and the really smart ones would try to hurt him beforehand.

Chase just smiled. "Look at the bright side, now there are more people for me to beat. And as a hero, I won't back down."

Drakonis smirked. "When the time comes, you must test your fate. Because a hero's place is never given, it's something you have to take." Isobel and Cyarah smiled. They both knew that Chase could do it no matter who he had to face.

Chase suddenly became serious. "Cyarah and Isobel, I have something that I have to ask you both. I need you both to go all out against me, because I have to be ready for anything that D'Merrion will throw at me." Isobel and Cyarah both smiled an evil smile. Drakonis grabbed the kids and made his way out of the building. When they were safely out, Drakonis turned toward the kids. "What else is there? I know that isn't the only news." All three of the children gave each other worried glances, then Dior spoke, "Word came from the storm division; Addurog will be participating."

Drakonis groaned. "Great. Just great, as if I don't have enough to worry about." Drakonis shook his head.

Everything was happening way too quickly and it was beginning to irritate him. He still had to search for the Manalourins and find out what they were up to. Drakonis could feel his anger rising; he needed to cool off. As if on cue, it began to rain. Drakonis looked up feeling the water droplets on his face; it was very relaxing. He looked to see the kids playing in the puddles. Drakonis sat and stared at the clouds. He watched the lightning dance across the sky as he was lost in thought. He didn't know how much time went by, but he was startled when he felt six people behind him. He turned to see Chase, Isobel, Cyarah and the kids standing behind him. Chase looked like he had gone through the netherworld and back, but Isobel and Cyarah looked much better. Chase extended his arm out toward Drakonis. Drakonis looked from Chase to his extended hand. Drakonis smirked as he grabbed it, and Chase pulled him to his feet.

Chase grinned. "Hey, Drakonis, I bet I can throw you a little bit farther now." Drakonis laughed, "I don't doubt it." Drakonis heard deep rumbling sounds, but he knew it wasn't the thunder because it sounded closer. He looked at the group behind him and everyone looked guilty.

"Come on, we are going to go get some food." Drakonis said.

As they were walking, Chase turned to Cyarah. "So, why were you so happy about getting the dragon's blood?"

Chase saw a sadistic grin cross Cyarah's face. "As you know, the dragons are almost extinct. And with the dragon's blood, I could recreate the whole species but Drakonis won't let me," she said with a pout. Isobel looked at Drakonis.

"Why wouldn't you want more of your kind running around?" Cyarah chuckled and answered, "Drakonis doesn't want a little brother or sister." They all looked at Drakonis to see if the statement was true.

"Dragons," he began, "Are not only prideful creatures, but they are also very powerful. If there were more of them, then there's no doubt that they'd rebel against father. Also; if my mother was to have another child that was a full-blooded dragon, then its power could rival mine."

Chase had a thoughtful expression. "But the dragons were wiped out by the previous divines, so they couldn't have been that strong." Drakonis chuckled, "You underestimate your predecessors. They were more powerful than you. But for some reason they became soft and they lost more and more battles. Saying that they were wiped out by the divines is wrong, because the dragon that was summoned did most of the work for them."

Cyarah glared at Drakonis. "Drakonis, I see that dragon pride you are referring to. We both know whoever your mother would choose to be with has to be more powerful than her. So, your little brother or sister would be just as powerful as you if not a little more."

Drakonis scoffed. "That's why I'm glad that they are pretty much extinct." Drakonis would never admit it, but Cyarah was partially right. The child could be just as powerful as him if trained properly.

Isobel started striding alongside Drakonis. "I'm sure that you don't actually mean that you're happy that they are almost gone?"

Drakonis looked at her from out of the corner of his eye. "There's always one in every race that will betray their own; and if I had to, I'd gladly make the dragon race extinct all over again." Cyarah looked at Drakonis with distaste in her eyes. "You're talking about Addurog and that dragon, aren't you?" Chase and Isobel both looked at each other; they actually knew Addurog and the dragon that they were referring to. At one point, they even fought Addurog. They only managed to escape, because they cut one of his wings off. Chase spoke up, "We've actually had to fight him before, but we don't know what he is."

Cyarah looked at the sky. "He was once a member of the proud phoenix race, whose power was on par with the dragons but the two races hated each other. Unlike the dragons, the phoenixes thought that killing humans was wrong. They were going to side with you, until they were betrayed by one of their own. Addurog was a phoenix who loved war, so he made a deal with D'Merrion. The deal was that if Addurog killed his race, then he would be made a god once D'Merrion was put back on the throne; that's exactly what Addurog did. He killed every one of his kind. But they cursed him, so he's a darker version of a phoenix and it pains him to come back to life. Besides dragons, Addurog hates humans a lot more."

Drakonis felt something really foreboding and it was eating him alive. "Cyarah, take Chase and Isobel back to the room. I'm going to take the kids back to King Maj." The seriousness in his voice put everyone on edge. Cyarah nodded and ushered Chase and Isobel toward their room. Drakonis turned with the children, and they started making their way to the Maj's chambers. Drakonis and the kids arrived at the chambers, and then he bent down and give all three a hug. Drakonis was walking back to his room, but he felt a presence approach him. As quickly as it came, it left. Drakonis walked into his room, and he saw everyone sitting there waiting for him.

Chase was the first to speak up. "So, do you and Addurog have a history?"

Drakonis thought for a moment, "We've had confrontations in the past. Just scuffles here and there, but nothing too serious. The thing is dragons and phoenixes are both dominate creatures. And if they are near each other, one has to dominate the other. I always beat Addurog; never once has he won."

It was Cyarah who spoke next, "You need to watch yourself, Drakonis. You and I both know that after what you did to his fallen brethren, he'll attempt to attack you anyway he can." Cyarah got up and walked toward the door,

"I'll be back in the morning to continue to help Chase train." With that said, she closed the door and left. Drakonis sighed.

He knew he was probably playing a dangerous game.

Isobel looked concerned. "Drakonis, if a phoenix can revive after dying, how can we permanently kill them?" Drakonis suddenly became very serious and said, "We killed them and gathered their ashes. And when they rose, we froze them since that is when they are at their weakest."

Chase looked hopeful. "So, where exactly did you put them after you froze them?"

Drakonis chuckled. "Looking for allies anywhere you can get them, huh?"

Chase shrugged pretending not to know what he was talking about.

"Even if you found where they were, it wouldn't matter because I stole their souls. They're just lifeless corpses right now. Look guys, it's been a long day. Why don't we get some rest for tomorrow?" Everyone nodded and went their separate ways unprepared for what was to come. Cyarah and Lydia made their way back to her room, when she had noticed a shadowy figure lurking behind her.

Cyarah calmly turned to face it. "You and I both know that you can't beat Drakonis so this petty feud will only end badly for you." The giant figure laughed a sinister laugh and said, "Alright." Cyarah replied, "It's your funeral." She began to walk into her room leaving the creature to itself. She saw the shadow of a person standing in her room. The figure walked toward her, "Cyarah, my dear, walk with me.

I need you to do something for me." Cyarah nodded. "What can I do for you, Lord D'Merrion?"

Chapter 9
Ten Days until the Crucible

The next morning, Chase and Isobel wandered out of their room. They looked at each other and then around the room. Drakonis was nowhere to be seen. Isobel walked toward the table and saw a note with food next to it. Isobel read the note then turned toward Chase.

"Drakonis said, D'Merrion called him early this morning and that we should go to the training room where we were yesterday. He said that Cyarah would be there to greet us." Chase nodded. They quickly ate their Breakfast, got dressed and began to head out. When they left their rooms, they were making their way throughout the building until Isobel stopped.

"Chase, "she said looking around. "Do you feel them surrounding us?" Chase nodded, but neither of them had any weapons. This was going to be difficult. Suddenly, a dozen creatures were surrounding them. They were six-foot-tall humanoid birds, and they were all armed to the teeth. Isobel and Chase stood back to back.

Isobel grinned. "It's been awhile since we have been able to fight side by side, huh Chase?" Chase smirked. "Yup, this is going to be a lot of fun." The bird like creatures charged at Isobel and Chase, but they rushed forward fighting like two people who've trained together their whole lives. The more birds they defeated, the more that came crawling out of the wood work. A whistling sound went out, and all the creatures stopped. The one that stood out above the others walked forth; he stood at least fifteen feet tall. The creature's face was of a bird. Its long feathery mane covered its entire neck and stopped at the top of its spine. The creature's colors were brownish red, but its helmet was of gold. It had a robe that covered its lower half, and this allowed its muscular upper half to be shown to the world. It was none other than Addurog himself. The giant creature began to speak in a deep voice.

"Imagine my surprise when I learned that the ones responsible for cutting one of my wings off were at the capital. Now, you're both going to help me capture Drakonis."

Isobel and Chase both chuckled. "Has losing your wing made you senile? Why would we help you?" Addurog laughed and snapped his fingers. All of a sudden more creatures came out holding Cyarah, Semaj, Mahogany and Dior.

"Now will you comply?"

Isobel and Chase looked at each other, and then back at Addurog.

"What is it you want?" They both said. Addurog grinned; and before anyone knew it, the two knights were lying unconscious on the ground. Addurog turned to one of his men.

"Tie them up and bring them with us, leave the Maj here. We need him to bring Drakonis to us." The creature nodded, Semaj watched as one of the creatures untied him and threw him to the ground.

"Run little boy," Addurog said. What he didn't expect was for Semaj to stand up and glare at him. "What are you going to do little boy, fight me?" Addurog said mocking him. Semaj still stood his ground, "Drakonis always said to stand up to protect those close to me, so I will protect them." Addurog glared down at the young prince. Semaj was scared, but he didn't back down. Addurog grinned. "There are moments in time when being tough will get you hurt." Addurog turned toward his men, "Show him men that this is one of those times." His men nodded and walked towards Semaj. Dior and Mahogany had tears streaming down their faces, as they watched the beasts brutally beat up Semaj. "When you get done, meet us at the rendezvous point."

With that said, Addurog and the rest of his men left to prepare for the next phase of their plan. Semaj lay bruised and beaten on the ground. He felt something licking him, so he opened a bruised eye and saw Lydia licking his wounds.

"Lydia," he said with a pained voice, "Take me to Drakonis." Lydia carefully picked up Semaj and placed him on her back. She began running down different hallways searching for Drakonis. But she suddenly picked up his scent, and she dashed toward it as quickly as she could. Drakonis was coming out of a meeting with his father. He had called him earlier that morning to talk to him about useless stuff. Drakonis suddenly heard something running towards him. He saw that it was Lydia with something on her back. When she stopped, he saw that it was Semaj but he wasn't moving. He ran towards Maj and saw that he was beaten and bruised, "Semaj," he said worriedly, "Who did this?" "Addurog, he took everyone else captive, and he's after you." Semaj whispered, barely conscious. Drakonis picked up Semaj and dashed toward the forgery with Lydia in tow. When he got there, he saw King Maj telling the other Majes how to do something. King Maj turned to Drakonis with a smile that instantly turned to a worried look when he saw his son in Drakonis' arms. Not a word was said when Drakonis handed him the child in his arms.

Drakonis turned to Lydia. "Take me to Addurog." Lydia nodded, understanding what he had said. Drakonis hopped on her back as she began to track Addurog.

Isobel looked up still groggy from being knocked unconscious. She then noticed that she was tied to a podium. She looked around and noticed that Chase was still coming to, and Mahogany, Dior and Cyarah were looking at Addurog who was barking orders at his men.

He turned towards them. "Good to see that you both are awake."

Cyarah narrowed her eyes. "Addurog, I can understand that you have a vendetta against Drakonis but beating Semaj to near death was a mistake that I fear you won't live to regret." Addurog seemed to ignore her warnings. He knew what he was doing. He was going to make Drakonis pay. Dior glared at Addurog, "Drakonis is going to make you pay for hurting Semaj!" Addurog growled and grabbed her by the neck. "Silence child unless you want to be next. The Maj prince will live but you're fully human, so I can snap your neck right now!" Addurog tightened his grip on her throat. Everyone was yelling for him to stop before he killed her. All of sudden, they heard a loud crashing sound. Everyone turned towards the noise and saw Drakonis standing there with his sword drawn and covered in blood.

Addurog smiled. "So the great half breed graces us with his presence."

Drakonis looked around the giant room and saw that there were a lot of soldiers waiting to see what he'd do. "Listen up! You're all soldiers, so your loyalty to Addurog is admirable. However, I'm giving you this one chance to leave and continue living your lives. But if you choose to stay, then you will die." No one moved a muscle. They all knew what he was capable of, but they ignored him.

"Mahogany and Dior, Semaj is alright but right now I need you both to close your eyes and not to open them until I say so." Said Drakonis with anger radiating from his body.

Isobel whispered to Cyarah. "Do you see Drakonis' face? He looks terrifying."

Cyarah nodded. "I've heard about him getting like this, but I've never seen it myself." Isobel remembered when she had hurt his grandfather, and he killed everyone but her.

Everyone felt a wave of mana pass through them.

Addurog whistled. "Wow, Drakonis, to have extended your mana field so far then you must be pretty serious."

Chase nudged Cyarah. "What's a mana field?"

"It's a dome of pure dark mana that Drakonis exerts from his body. Since dark mana can't be used like normal mana, Drakonis uses his body as a conduit. In doing so, anything that is inside the field Drakonis is in. Drakonis can practically feel what they're going to do which allows him to react even faster than normal. He usually keeps it within arm's length and calls it his mana field." Chase and Isobel watched in awe. What was the extent of Drakonis' power? Many of the soldiers began to rush at Drakonis only to be cut down. Drakonis continued to stare at Addurog, because he was the one he was after and his little minions were nothing more than cannon fodder. As he got closer to Addurog, he suddenly felt himself get wrapped up in chains. Addurog started laughing like a madman.

"Seems as though you've fallen into my trap; not even you can break those bonds. They restrict any kind of mana including yours." Drakonis looked down at the chains and then back at Addurog. Drakonis added a lot of pressure to the chains, and they snapped. Addurog watched wide eyed.

"How did you do that? Those chains restrict any kind of mana!"

Drakonis gave a dark chuckle. "I'm glad that my strength isn't considered a form of mana." Addurog was sweating bullets. "Look, Drakonis, I'm sorry. There are no hard feelings, you know? Please let me live."

Drakonis shook his head. "Pathetic, but I've already decided I'm going to end you." Addurog got on his knees. "I'm sorry, please forgive me. I won't ever do it again!" Drakonis barely caught Addurog's smirk, before he brought his sword up in time to block Addurog's sword.

Addurog grinned. "Did you really think I'd just let you win?" Addurog's sword was a giant seven-foot-long great sword that was all a dark gold with glowing runes inscribed into it. Drakonis and Addurog began to clash. Despite the size difference, they were going toe to toe in blows.

Chase noticed something was off. "Do you both see those cracks in Drakonis' sword?" Isobel and Cyarah nodded. Whatever Addurog's sword was made of was stronger than dragon scales. Drakonis narrowed his eyes. He had noticed the cracks himself, because not many things could actually crack dragon scales. Their fight continued, but it seemed more and more like Addurog was winning.

Drakonis growled an animalistic growl. His dragon's blood was boiling to the point where he was seeing red.

Addurog's sinister grin grew. "How does it feel half breed? How does it feel to be brought to your knees by a superior race? How does it feel?" Drakonis felt his sword shatter before it even happened. He looked wide eyed at the remains of his sword. Addurog put his sword on his shoulder. "What now, Drakonis? Your little knife is broken, and you can't use magic because the sentries will come. But instead of killing you, I guess I'll just kill your friends." Addurog turned and hurled his sword toward the tied-up onlookers. Drakonis snapped out of his shock and dashed towards the sword. As soon as he grabbed the sword, he felt a searing pain in his body. During that time, Addurog grabbed Drakonis by the neck and said, "Time to squeeze the life out of you." Addurog tightened his grip around Drakonis neck. "Enough!" everyone turned to see D'Merrion standing in the entrance of the building, "Addurog! You've proven your point. You can leave." Addurog growled but dropped Drakonis. Then he gathered his men and left the building.

"Drakonis, I'm really disappointed in you. You could have killed him if you wanted to, but you wanted to save them. This was a test we orchestrated, and you failed. You may not have known this, but Addurog is trying to take your place as the guardian of the capital. Seeing how he almost killed you, I'm really starting to agree to it." D'Merrion turned and left. Drakonis got up, walked toward the group that was tied up and broke their chains.

He then turned toward Cyarah and got in her face, "Did you know about this?"

"Drakonis." Chase said, but Drakonis ignored him.

"Cyarah, did you know about this?" Chase grabbed Drakonis and pulled him away. "Why would she have been tied up with us if she knew?"

Cyarah put her hand on Chase's shoulder. "Yes, Drakonis, I did know about it. D'Merrion told me about it last night." Everyone except Drakonis looked shocked. "However, I did not know how they were going to do things. I didn't know that they were going to hurt Semaj, nor did I know about Addurog's new weapon." Drakonis turned toward Mahogany and Dior who still had their eyes closed. He threw both of them over his shoulder and began walking toward the exit. Chase looked back toward Cyarah "So, why didn't you tell us? What do you get out of it?!" Cyarah didn't seem fazed by his outburst. She just said, "What I got out of it is none of your business." Chase shook his head. "We trusted you, and you sold us out but for what?"

Cyarah narrowed her eyes at him. "Don't play me for a fool. You two have been here for weeks, and we've magically gained your trust. I wouldn't have lived this long if I didn't know the rules of the game." Cyarah turned and walked out refusing to say anything else. Isobel put her hand on Chase's shoulder "Come on Chase, let's go find Drakonis and the kids." Chase nodded but didn't say a word. Isobel picked up the remains of Drakonis' sword; and with that, they dashed out of the room quickly trying to find the forge. When they got there, they saw Drakonis, King Maj and a doctor standing over Semaj. The doctor smiled at them, but then looked back at King Maj.

"Good thing you brought him when you did. We gave him the medicine, so all you need to do is make sure he isn't doing anything too strenuous." King Maj nodded to the man, and looked back at his child.

"Drakonis, I want to know what happened." Drakonis looked at the man then back at the child. "This was all a test that D'Merrion set up for me, and I failed." King Maj's eyes widened then he noticed that something was wrong with Drakonis "Drakonis, where is your sword?" Drakonis didn't even make eye contact with the king. Isobel walked up with the broken weapon in her hand, and gave it to the king. King Maj was beyond surprised. He was astonished that something could break one of his best weapons.

"Who did this?" the words barely came out as a whisper.

Chase was the one to speak. "Addurog, and his new weapon. It broke through Drakonis' sword like it was nothing."

King Maj shook his head. "What sort of weapon could just cut through this so easily?" A new voice was heard.

"Apparently, a weapon made from light and darkness."

Everyone turned to see Cyarah walking in with Lydia behind her. Drakonis growled, "What are you doing here?" Cyarah did not seem fazed. "I don't care how you feel toward me. But you helped me at one point in time, so now I have to help you." She turned toward Lydia and took the bag that she had in her mouth. "In this bag is a new element that Addurog discovered. From what I could gather, when Drakonis frenzied his godlike power may have unknowingly created it. It's called Chrocosium." Chase was shaking his head in denial. "That's not even possible."

Cyarah scoffed. "We live in a world with gods, demons, dragons and everything else that walked upon this planet, but you say it's impossible to create new elements." Chase looked away as his face reddened.

Cyarah handed the ore to Drakonis. "This is all that remains of that powerful element. I'm giving it to you, so you can make another weapon for yourself that will be even more powerful than your last." Cyarah turned and walked out. A small smile was on Chase's face. Drakonis handed the king of the Majes the ore. "I can't ask you to stop watching over your child to build me a weapon; but if you can at any point in time, then I'd be forever in your debt." King Maj looked at the ore and then back at Drakonis. "All I want is for you to crush Addurog. I want you to tear him apart. I want him to know to never to mess with us again." Drakonis smirked and bowed his head. "I will destroy him entirely, so that he knows never to do it again." Isobel pondered something for a moment.

"Drakonis, you said that the women of the Majes can sense when their children are in danger. So wouldn't

Semaj's mom have sensed that beforehand and contacted either of you about it?"

King Maj nodded in agreement. "I thought about that earlier, so I attempted to contact the Stealth brigade but they wouldn't respond. We will have to wait until Azzaria gets here since my wife is a part of her personal guard."

Drakonis agreed. "Apparently, Addurog wants my position as the defender of the capital. If I can't somehow prove to my father that I'm capable of keeping this position..."

Chase looked at him. "Do you know how you're going to do that?"

Drakonis shook his head. "I'll cross that bridge when I get to it." Drakonis began to walk out with Isobel and Chase in tow. As they made their way throughout the castle, they were being questioned by almost everyone about what had happened. With one glare from Drakonis, everyone was sent scurrying off. Before Isobel or Chase could ask where they were going, they pushed through some giant doors.

Xinovioc was staring down at Addurog. The dragon stood on his hind legs and stared down at the creature before him.

"You hurt Drakonis or those children again, and you'll definitely regret it." Addurog scoffed and made his way out of the dragon's room. Drakonis walked up to his grandfather, "Grandfather if you wouldn't mind, let's go for a flight." The dragon smiled and nodded. He bent down and picked up the trio and put them on his back. Xinovioc walked toward the door that led outside; and once there, he took off into the sky. He was doing all sorts of stunts much to the delight of those on his back. Drakonis looked back at Isobel and Chase.

"Hold on," he said. Xinovioc started to climb higher and higher into the sky. When he finally leveled, Drakonis stood up, "Ready, grandfather?" The dragon nodded. Isobel and Chase watched as Drakonis jumped off of his grandfather and started diving. Xinovioc turned to his last few passengers, "I feel bad for him, to have the blood of a dragon but not the wings. A dragon needs the wind like a fish needs water. Many of my brothers would have probably killed themselves, but not him." Before anyone could respond, Xinovioc went into a dive. He quickly swooped under Drakonis allowing him to land on his grandfather's back. Drakonis looked back. "Who wants to go next?" He was met with blank looks. Drakonis just shrugged, "Grandfather, we've got some unwilling passengers."

Before anyone could retort, the dragon turned upside down which caused everyone to start falling. Isobel and Chase began to yell at Drakonis for dropping them. When Xinovioc finally caught them, the duo were screaming death threats at Drakonis for having his grandfather drop them. When they finally landed, the sun had set and the stars were shining in the sky. Drakonis thanked his grandfather for the flight. They made their way back to the room that they all shared. When they opened the door, they saw a full array of food on the table with a note telling them that it was from King Maj. As they began to eat, Chase looked toward Drakonis. "So,

Drakonis, what are you going to do about Addurog?" Drakonis was thoughtful for a moment.

"What I want to do is erase him from the entire plain of existence, but I'm going to have to beat him so my father won't change our positions." Isobel looked at him from the corner of her eye. "Is it part of the revenge for him beating you, or is it for what he did to the kids?"

Drakonis scoffed. "You make it seem like revenge is bad?"

Isobel was surprised at what Drakonis said. "Revenge is never the way to go; it only brings about despair."

Drakonis chuckled. "You forget that I am in despair. When people see me, they run because I bring about destruction. However, people only see the negative of revenge. It means to exact punishment, and I will exact punishment but that has to come later. I need something to happen to make my father lose trust in Addurog. We should get some sleep; we don't know what tomorrow is going to bring us. I'm going to sleep in the garden." With that said, Drakonis left the room. Isobel looked at Chase. "I guarantee you that Drakonis is a lot angrier than he lets on." Chase let out a soft chuckle. "It doesn't surprise me. Drakonis is a person of immeasurable power, and he was beaten by someone who he's previously beaten numerous times. Then Addurog had the nerve to hurt one of the closest things to Drakonis. If he wasn't mad, then something would probably be wrong with him. I'm going to turn in for the night." Chase waved as he went in his room. Isobel sat there and contemplated everything Chase had said to her, and he was right. Drakonis is half dragon, and dragons have issues with their pride. Isobel felt a familiar presence. She looked toward the balcony and saw a figure surrounded by shadows. Isobel sighed to herself and walked toward the balcony. When she opened the door, she saw Ariel. "Greetings princess," he said with a toothy grin. Isobel smirked. "I think the gods are displeased with me seeing as though they allowed the likes of you to grace my presence." Ariel frowned. "To think, I was coming here to help you with your bird problem." With this, Ariel knew he had her attention, "It doesn't matter how I know, but what I do know is that Drakonis needs to get back into favor with his father. I think I may have an idea on how to do such a thing. D'Merrion is not only a god, but a god that loves the things he's collected. Addurog is going to be head of security for D'Merrion's annual parade. It's when he gets in a carriage and goes throughout the city to meet his people. It'd be a shame if something happened to him." Isobel had thoughtful expression on her face. "What is it you're after Ariel?" He smiled. "You of course. But since it'd be a lot more work to take you, then I'll just settle for your mana." Isobel eyed him warily. "You're smarter than you look. Is my mana so delicious that you'd risk your life for it?" Ariel simply nodded.

"I don't trust you. I know you're hiding something, but desperate times call for desperate measures. So, how do you plan on taking my mana?" Ariel grinned for ear to ear. Ariel grabbed Isobel and pulled her into a kiss. Isobel was about to retaliate, but then felt most of her mana disappear almost instantly. When Ariel separated from her, she glared daggers at him. "You ever do that again, and I'll cut your head off." Ariel laughed. "Aww, princess was that your first kiss?" Isobel cocked back her fist and punched him in the jaw. Ariel staggered for a minute, then he rubbed his jaw. "I thought your strength was enhanced by your mana, but I was wrong. Anyway, you should probably distract Drakonis for a few days." With that, Ariel disappeared off the balcony leaving Isobel to her thoughts. She felt a set of eyes staring into the back of her head. She turned to see Chase standing there watching her with wary eyes. "So, what was that about?"

Isobel chuckled nervously. "Well you see. He came around here once before, but I completely forgot about it. Now, he says he can help get Drakonis back into favor with D'Merrion." Chase nodded. "Now Isobel, I know you're capable of making your own decisions, but you're making a deal with the devil. I think you should tell Drakonis about this." Isobel nodded. "It would probably be a good idea after Ariel does what he needs to do." Chase nodded while he closed his door and proceeded back to bed. Isobel walked to her room, laid down, closed her eyes and waited for what was to come.

Chapter 10
Three days until the Crucible

Isobel didn't need to distract Drakonis. Because for days since the incident happened, his time had been occupied with training nonstop. She'd never seen him like this. Instead of wearing the clothes with encryptions that increase the gravity on your body, he used rings; he had one for each finger.

At first, he couldn't move. But over time, he was running laps around the whole city. He would go to building sites and lift things that weighed tons. It was terrifying. But to increase his mana reserve, he'd push his dark mana field as far out as he could as often as he could. He had worked on every aspect of his being. Chase and Isobel watched as Drakonis was doing pushups while in a handstand. Chase looked at Isobel. "So, when is this thing that your friend has agreed to help you with supposed to start?" Isobel shrugged; she herself didn't know the answer to that. Everyone heard a familiar hissing sound coming up behind them. They turned to see Cyarah coming up to them. "Drakonis, King Maj has requested your presence in the forge." Drakonis looked at her and nodded. He finished his workout and wiped his brow with his towel.

"Come on guys, let's see what the King has in store for us." As they made their way to the forge, a certain number of things caught everyone's eyes. First, there were a large number of Addurog's lackey's patrolling the streets. Secondly, Lydia had wings. Thirdly, Cyarah was dressed as a civilian and not as a mad scientist. Chase broke the silence.

"So Cyarah, how have you been?" Cyarah didn't even bother to respond to him; she didn't care for small talk. Lydia looked back at Drakonis and made an assortment of noises.

Drakonis' eyes widened ever so slightly. "So Cyarah, I'm going to go out on a limb here and say that you injected Lydia with the dragon DNA which gave her wings." Cyarah scoffed. "I wonder what gave that away," she said

rhetorically. Drakonis smirked. "That and the fact that she just said you feel upset about betraying us, but you're too stubborn to apologize." Cyarah stopped and looked from Lydia to Drakonis.

"Can you understand her?" she said with a surprised face." Drakonis chuckled. "I wonder what gave that away." They had finally reached the forge when a large explosion went off; blowing many Majes out of the room. The group rushed inside to see King Maj lying face down on the ground. Drakonis ran toward the king and turned him over, only to be met with a devilish grin. King Maj jumped to his feet. "Hello everyone, glad you could make it." He said sounding almost too excited. He turned and walked toward the center of the room which looked as if it was where the explosion first went off. Everyone looked at the crater in the room to see two swords lying parallel to one another. King Maj picked them up and made sure to hold them apart.

"I'm ecstatic to unveil my newest creations." He lifted up one of the swords; it was as white as snow. The carvings in the blade were magnificent; the hilt was made of diamond. The blade itself looked weak, but anyone could tell it could that it could only be matched by a few blades in the world. King Maj smiled. "This is Rohaz the sword of light, and this is Rajani the sword of darkness." He put down Rohaz and held up the other sword which was completely black. It seemed as if it could cut through darkness itself. It was completely identical to Rohaz, except for the color difference. King Maj put them both on a pedestal and continued with what he was going to say.

"They are twins. Drakonis step forward and reach out your hand." Drakonis did as he was told, but as he stuck out

131

his hand both swords began to shake. Finally, Rajani levitated over to Drakonis and landed in his hand. Drakonis instantly felt multiple presences in his mind. He attempted to let go of the sword, but it had already wrapped its hilt around his arm. Drakonis fell to his knees; it felt like there were millions of damned souls attempting to take over his mind. He could hear the faint voice of King Maj. "Drakonis, since she is a sword of darkness, she possesses the souls of the damned, and they will try to possess you but you have to overcome it." Drakonis nodded and sat on the ground in a meditating position. In his mind, he felt millions of souls trying to suppress him, but he wouldn't have it. Drakonis silenced the voices in his head all at once through sheer willpower. There was one voice left in his head, and it was soothing but it held a certain dark tone.

"I am the voice of the sword, Drakonis. You've proven yourself worthy of me for now. I hereby grant you the power I hold and the right to wield me." Drakonis opened his eyes to see everyone staring at him. King Maj examined him. "I see you're not foaming at the mouth, so that's good." Drakonis stood up and dusted himself off. "So, am I supposed to pick up Rohaz?" King Maj immediately pulled the other sword away, "No!" He shouted, "Under no circumstance are you to wield both swords at the same time." Drakonis nodded, not understanding why but he believed the king anyway. "So, what it is the other sword for?"

King Maj smiled. "Isobel, step forward and put your hand out." Everyone was shocked. Isobel was a little apprehensive about it, but she mustered up the courage to put her hand out. This sword; much like its twin, shook for a moment before levitating toward Isobel and landing in her hand. Before she blacked out, she heard King Maj say something to her. "Isobel, nothing you're about to experience will be real, but it will be hard for you to overcome." Isobel opened her eyes to see that she was sitting on a throne in a beautiful room. She looked around when suddenly the door burst open, and a young man walked in but he seemed angry.

"My queen, why did you deny the marriage contract between me and the one I love?" Isobel didn't know what to say. The man in front of her continued to rant on.

"You always said that I could choose the one who I would marry so I did, but you deny my request. Do you deny me as queen or as my selfish mother?" Isobel was taken aback. Was this her child? She had to think quickly.

133

"Remove your helmet, dear boy. Let me get a good look at you." The man in front of her sighed and took off his helmet. Isobel gasped, he was an exact replica of Drakonis.

"Drakonis, is that you?" The man in front of her stiffened and suddenly relaxed.

"No mom. Dad died, so that you could rule over all the gods." Isobel shook her head this had to be some sort of sick joke. The man continued. "You always went on about how much you both loved each other so much that he gave his life for you in the end, but it's really pathetic if you ask me."

Isobel went from shock to anger. "Don't you dare refer to your father like that; he's the only reason you're here today." The man scoffed and left the room. Isobel couldn't believe it. She left her throne room and ran through the hallway. She stopped when she saw someone who looked way too familiar. She ran up to the man. "Chase!" she yelled. The man looked at her and narrowed his eyes. Isobel for the second time today was taken aback.

"Chase, what's wrong?" Chase glared at her.

"Why you are talking to me? You refused to bring back Cyarah like you promised!" Isobel couldn't fathom what was going on. Chase saw her face and got angrier, "You don't remember when Cyarah died for you; allowing you to live? You promised me that when you were put on the throne you'd bring her back." Isobel watched the tears that streamed down Chase's face. Chase ran off leaving Isobel to her thoughts. She could only wonder what happened to make everyone the way they were. Isobel continued to walk throughout the castle. She wracked her brain for answers, but nothing came; only faint words from King Maj. Isobel brightened up, because she only needed to find King Maj. She ran around the castle looking for the Majes, but found no trace of them anywhere. She was out of options, and she felt like giving up. She then remembered that she never gave up no matter the circumstances; even when she foolishly fought Drakonis for the first time. Everything began to flow. Everything from the past was coming back to her memory. There was one thing in particular that stood out. King Maj was saying that it wasn't real. She began to run; her mind leading her to where she needed to be. She turned down a hallway to see a large number of people standing there and in front was Chase and her son. They were adamant on stopping her, because they knew she had no weapons. Isobel faced the small army with only her wits. "That's it!" She thought to herself. She needed a weapon, and she needed one fast. Isobel began to concentrate. What was the most powerful weapon she could think of? She heard another familiar voice, so she looked and there in front of her stood Drakonis. He turned and looked down at her and smiled.

"Long time, no see, what do you need me to do?" Isobel could almost see tears in her eyes. She hugged Drakonis adamant on not letting go. Drakonis was a little shocked, but hugged her back. "As much as I enjoy holding you, there's an army in front of us that doesn't look too pleased." She had completely forgotten about the army in front of her. Drakonis walked forward.

"So, before we start this, does anyone want to leave?" No one from the other army moved. Drakonis smiled and pulled out his sword.

"I'm glad none of you left, because it would have been less fun for me." Isobel looked at Drakonis. "I don't want you to kill them, just knock them out." Drakonis nodded. They stood next to each other and charged the army in front of them. Drakonis and Isobel began to fight in sync. It was like they did this every day. The army stood no chance against them. When they had finally finished knocking out the last of the army, Isobel looked forward and saw her way out but then she turned back towards Drakonis.

"I don't want to leave, but I have to." Drakonis walked up to her and kissed her forehead. Isobel instantly blushed, as she smiled back at Drakonis. She turned and kept walking down the hallway. As she kept walking, everything around disappeared. She suddenly appeared in a white room, and then she heard a voice full of light.

"You have passed our test young one. Go with our blessings and smite any who stands against you." Isobel opened her eyes, and saw everyone standing around her.

King Maj examined Isobel just as he did Drakonis.

"I see you actually woke up." Drakonis looked at King

Maj. "So, how did you know what was going to happen?" King Maj stroked his beard. "When I first began to craft those swords, Rajani pulled my conscious into the ore after I separated her from Rohaz; she read my thoughts. We came to an agreement that she would be able to test her new wielder in any way she saw fit. I agreed, and she told me how she'd test you but made me promise not to say anything. Rohaz did the exact same thing to me, but his test was a lot different from his twin sister. I asked them both what would happen if someone would try to dual wield them. They said that since they've been separated; that if someone tried to bring them that close again, it would destroy their mind and their bodies wouldn't be too far behind. The power you would wield would be incomprehensible, but at the cost of your very being. You can both duel each other. But neither of you cannot; I repeat, cannot wield both of these swords."

Drakonis and Isobel both nodded. King Maj then turned to Chase.

"Chase, I have a special surprise for you. Aviance is finally ready for you; but a word of advice, keep her hidden until you really need her." Aviance floated down toward Chase. "It's good to see you again. Chase. I do hope that we will work well together." Everyone heard loud music in the distance, and King Maj turned towards Drakonis.

"I see the festival is starting, but I'm surprised D'Merrion didn't have you in charge of security since you always make sure that things go without a hitch. Drakonis shrugged. "I don't really care, and if he wants Addurog to do it then by all means allow him to mess up." King Maj nodded in agreement. Drakonis' ear twitched as he started to hear screams. He alongside everyone else ran to where the sounds had originated. When they arrived, they saw a large group of people attacking Addurog and his troops. Drakonis quickly jumped into action, "King Maj, why aren't the sentinels coming out?" "Probably because the explosion destroyed the summoning runes in this area." King Maj yelled back over the screams of the people in the parade. Drakonis shouted to Cyarah. "Cyarah, take King Maj back to the forge and see what you can do about getting power to the sentinels. Chase and Isobel, let's see if we can help Addurog out." With that said, everyone began to do what they were ordered to do. Drakonis made sure to keep his rings on, and only to take them off in dire situations. Drakonis pulled out his new sword, and he forced his mana field out so that he could keep an eye on everything that was going on in the battle. Just as quickly as his mana field had appeared, it instantly disappeared. Drakonis felt all of the dark mana he had just used flow into his sword. Drakonis heard the sword in his thoughts.

"Yes, feed us more with your dark power, and we will make all bow before you. But be warned, when you run out of dark mana we will consume you. Now wield us, and smite down your enemies." Drakonis knew he and the sword were probably going to clash at one point, but right now he needed to fight. Drakonis swung his sword at the nearest enemy. He was surprised when a purplish demonic serpent erupted from his sword and wrapped itself around the soldier. The creature opened its jaw and began to consume the man. Drakonis watched as the man was dissipated only leaving the man's soul. Drakonis was disturbed when the serpent began to consume the man's soul. Chase looked at Drakonis, "That's really disturbing even for King Maj." Drakonis shrugged; but when he looked around, they were surrounded by enemy soldiers. Isobel smiled. She could only wonder what her sword was capable of. She swung her sword, and a fiery red bird exploded from it and flew through the enemies surrounding them turning them into ash. Isobel felt her mana drain, but not as much as when Ariel kissed her. Chase felt a rush of energy from seeing what Drakonis and Isobel could do.

He said, "Aviance dual swords." Aviance immediately transformed into two silver swords. Chase dashed toward the remaining enemies, and his sword's play was like a dance of death. Chase hadn't felt such a rush in a long time. He blocked, parried and slashed his enemies. Chase was enjoying himself to say the least. When he finally finished his deadly dance, his enemies laid in a pool of their own blood. Drakonis whistled, "I severely underestimated you." Everyone turned to see Addurog cutting down enemies. Isobel recognized Ariel and his

Manalourins attacking D'Merrion. But instead of striking D'Merrion, Ariel stole the crown off of D'Merrion's head. As soon as he had it, Ariel shouted to the rest of his forces to retreat. They ran to the nearest sewer and dived in. D'Merrion yelled to Drakonis to get his crown back. Drakonis nodded.

"Come on, you two." They all reached the sewer, and jumped in. As they got inside, Drakonis tried to extend his mana field, but only to have his mana eaten by his sword. Drakonis groaned as this would be a problem down the line. It felt as though they were walking for hours. Drakonis felt as if something was suffocating him. He looked around, but only saw darkness and it was constricting him. He noticed the dark aura surrounding him and his sword.

"Rajani," he said confused and annoyed. "Why does it feel like the darkness in this sewer is trying to constrict me?" He could hear faint laughing; the serpent looked Drakonis in the eye. "The darkness consumes all, and we want your soul." Drakonis let out a dark chuckle. "I'd be impressed, but you disappoint me. Your efforts are in vain, because I don't have a soul." The serpent was perplexed. How could she have never noticed? She was too busy trying to consume souls, and take over Drakonis' body. The snake hissed at him. "This isn't over." Drakonis looked at the sword; it had stopped pulsing. He felt Isobel's arm on his shoulder. He looked back at her as she pointed behind them. He noticed that they were surrounded; but not by people, they were surrounded by giant rats. They looked like body builders, but they had parts of their skin missing which revealed their innards. Isobel shuddered while looking at the rats; disgusting wasn't even the word to use in this situation.

"Hey guys" Chase said gaining everyone's attention. He pointed in front of the sewer which was being blocked by more man sized rodents. Isobel shook her head. "Nope, you both can deal with these creatures; I refuse to fight them." Drakonis and Chase both gave her a blank look.

"What?" she said glaring at them both, "This is disgusting, even for me." Chase shook his head, and then looked at Drakonis. "I'll take the ones behind, and you take the ones in front." Drakonis turned toward the large group of super rats in front of him. He pulled out Rajani. He cut the first creature, but he noticed that the creature wasn't affected. He looked at his sword and was surprised to see that it was dull. He growled in annoyance. He hadn't even known the stupid weapon for more than a day, and it was already pissing him off. He sheathed his sword deciding that hand to hand combat would better suit him. The rats were using their giant claws to try and cut up Drakonis. He dodged and swayed each one noticing that they were faster than he was expecting. Drakonis looked back to see Chase enjoying himself with his assortment of weapons. He gazed over at Isobel to see her looking at him with worry in her eyes.

Drakonis turned back toward the creatures in front of him. He proceeded to pierce one of them through the heart with his hand; but instead of normal red blood, a black liquid was on his hand. He was too busy trying to find out what was on his hand to notice that another creature had bitten into his arm. Drakonis hissed in pain as the creature threw him into the air. Drakonis spun and put his foot into the creature's head on his way back down; instantly crushing it. He looked at his arm to see the same black liquid seeping off his armor; its teeth had barely pierced his armor. Drakonis turned back to the other creatures. He was tired of toying with them. He stuck his arm out and a red ball appeared in his hand. Drakonis narrowed his eyes at the creatures and uttered one word, "Burn." A large wave of fire exploded from Drakonis' hand incinerating everything in his path. He heard whistling behind him, and he turned to see Chase sitting next to Isobel.

"For as long as I've known you, I haven't seen you use magic like that." Chase said standing up, and Isobel nodded in agreement. Drakonis started walking down the hallway.

"I haven't used magic like that since my first run with the Manalourins. What about you both?" They both looked at him with annoyed looks. "Drakonis," Isobel said, "Remember when you said using magic would get us in trouble?" Isobel glanced at Drakonis then his sword. "So what happened with Rajani, and what's that black gunk on your arm?" Drakonis pulled his sword back out to see that it was still dull.

"Apparently, this sword was trying to consume my soul. But got mad that she couldn't, so she's getting her revenge against me but I'm not telling her that. Also; this gooey stuff, I think I know what it is but we will have to find out later." They all continued to walk until they entered what looked like a giant dark cavern. Drakonis stopped. "Anyone else get the feeling that we are being watched?" The two people behind him nodded their head. Isobel swung her sword into the air releasing the firebird to illuminate the room, and what they saw was disheartening. They were surrounded by more giant rats. But instead of a few, there were dozens. They heard a maniacal laugh coming from above them, and they looked up to see Ariel standing on a platform. Before he could speak, Isobel interrupted him.

"Ariel, what in all the god's names is this?" Ariel gave her a confused look, so she sighed and pointed to the giant rodents.

"What are these?" Ariel chuckled, "These are some of the newest members of my army. I've created them by infusing them with dark mana and forced them to do my bidding.

The reason I've chosen these creatures is because there's so many of them in the sewer." Drakonis eyed both Isobel and this new person named Ariel; the name sounded oddly familiar. Drakonis gazed at Isobel.

"So, who is this clown?" Ariel ignored Drakonis' jab at him. "I'm the man who's taken Isobel's innocence." Drakonis raised a brow. "Hopefully, you didn't do that in my room." Ariel had a smug look on his face. "Yes, I enjoyed it very much, and Isobel was so very flustered; it was adorable." Drakonis glanced back at Isobel to be greeted by her angry face, but there was a small blush on her checks. There was a crackling of lightning behind them. Drakonis turned to see Chase standing there with his fists clenched and an aura of lightning surrounding him.

Drakonis stepped aside, as Chase dashed past him and up the wall toward where Ariel stood.

"Aviance power gauntlets!" he yelled. Aviance transformed in pair of black gauntlets with spikes on the knuckles. Chase made his way toward Ariel only to be blocked by more mutated rats.

"Out of my way!" Chase yelled quickly and dispatched the creatures, only to be blocked by more of them. As Chase crushed his enemies, Drakonis focused his attention on Isobel.

"So, do you care to explain?" The blush on her face deepened.

"He's technically my first kiss, but then again he isn't. When I kissed you on the cheek was my first, but I don't know if that counts." Drakonis snickered.

"If it makes you feel better, then I'll allow myself to count as your first kiss." Isobel giggled, but then stopped. She looked to see Chase almost getting to Ariel, only to be knocked away by someone who appeared next to Ariel. Chase landed next to Isobel and Drakonis; they all glared at the new comer. It was another Manalourin; he was the same size as Chase, but he wore a mask to cover his face. You could see clearly into his eyes, and he was staring directly at Chase. Ariel glanced at the newcomer. "Zavire, since you're here why don't you take Chase, I see you itching to get to him." Chase cracked his knuckles. "I've been itching to cut loose." The lightning around him crackled even more. The Manalourin pulled out what looked like a sword with a spiked ball chain at the end. Chase raised a brow. "Aviance, dual sword." Aviance turned into gold twin katana's. Zavire jumped off a platform toward Chase. Their swords clashed which created a shockwave around them. Isobel walked past Drakonis.

"You don't mind if I take Ariel, do you? I really want some payback, plus I don't want to fight these rats." Drakonis glared at her, "I don't think so." Isobel thought for a moment, she then walked up and planted a kiss on Drakonis cheek.

"Please." Isobel said giving him her best puppy pout. Drakonis didn't bother looking at her after the kiss.

"Fine, go ahead." Isobel laughed and jumped toward Ariel. Drakonis looked around to see all the giant rodents surrounding him. He sighed; this was going to be a while. Chase was matching blows with Zavire. Something about this man wasn't right. He ducked right before the spiked ball could hit him in the face. Sparks flew as their swords crossed once again. The man began to chuckle as they kept trading blows. Finally getting tired of it, Chase decided to humor him.

"What's so funny?" The man pointed behind Chase.

"Yea right, like I'm going to be stupid enough to look behind me." Suddenly, Chase felt something cut his side. He looked down to see another spiked ball chain wrapping itself around him. Chase felt himself being lifted up into the air and thrown into a wall. As he stood up, he saw what could only be another Manalourin walking and swinging their swords that also had spiked ball chains. Chase stood watching as the two creatures started walking towards him. Chase charged himself with lightning again, this time increasing his speed. The two Manalourins charged at him, but Chase smiled on the inside because these guys weren't as strong as Cyarah individually but together they could match her. "Aviance, chain sickles." Aviance glowed, then turned into two miniature scythes connected by one chain. Chase held one by the handle but was spinning the other by the chain. Suddenly, an explosion rocked the underground cavern. Chase burst out laughing, as he saw Isobel beating up Ariel. He turned back to the Manalourins only to see that they were gone. He felt two chains wrap around him, and he looked back as they tightened the chains on him. It felt as though they were trying to crush him, so he had to think quickly. He got an idea, and he gathered up his lightning mana. He set it through the chains that were holding him, and the effects were instant. There was a large amount of electricity that shot through them causing them to collapse. Chase gave himself a pat on the back, but then he thought about something. Why didn't he knock them out at the beginning of the fight? He shrugged his shoulders. He'd leave that part out of the story when he was going to tell Cyarah. Then out of the blue, he felt something on his neck. So he reached up, took whatever pierced his neck and gently pulled it out. It was a sleeping dart. He looked around to see another hooded figure with a gun pointed at him. Chase felt his eyes get heavy. He tried to walk, but his legs were already asleep. He didn't have any choice, but to fall over and accept the wave of drowsiness that overcame him.

Isobel was busy fighting Ariel. He was a slippery one. But the moment she got her hands on him, she began to beat his face in. She had thrown him into the wall causing it to collapse on him. Ariel rose out of the rubble and started to dust himself off. He pulled out two guns from nowhere and grinned when Isobel noticed she didn't have her sword, so she could only dodge. Isobel jumped back in order to ready a spell. She stopped when a bullet grazed her ear, but she noticed they weren't bullets but darts. She gasped when she realized that they were sleeping darts.

"Heavenly chains!" She yelled, suddenly. Golden chains shot from the ground beneath Ariel's feet wrapping themselves around him. Before she could follow up, a chain wrapped around her arms. She looked to see where it was coming from; it was Zavire and two other Manalourins. She looked back at Ariel who was making his way toward her.

"It's been a while since I've had some of your mana.

I guess it wouldn't harm me to take more of it." Isobel glared at him, but then she saw a black blur fly toward her; she quickly grabbed it. It was Drakonis' sword. She looked over to see him go back to fighting the endless number of mutated rodents. She used the sword to cut the chains and then turned back toward Ariel.

"Rajani, I know you probably want to test me to see if I'm worthy of you, but I ask that you save that for later and help me win this fight." The sword shook in her hand, so Isobel took that as an agreement. She could feel the dark mana that was held inside the sword, and she suddenly had a great idea.

"Rajani; in whatever direction I swing you, I want you to release a wave of dark mana and I'll replace it all later."

Isobel swung the sword toward Ariel, but at first nothing had happened. Then a giant surge of dark mana was released from the sword right toward Ariel. He had no way to dodge and was hit in his chest. The blow sent him flying. Isobel smiled to herself feeling very proud. She turned toward the other Manalourins, who had surrounded and noticed that they were all pointing guns at her. Her eyes widened as they all began to shoot at her. She began to deflect most of them; but before she knew it, there were some sticking out of different parts of her armor. All of a sudden, she felt something hit the back of her neck. She turned around to see Ariel bleeding profusely, but he still had enough energy to point a gun at her. Isobel felt the effects immediately. She fell to her knees still holding onto Rajani for dear life. She saw Ariel standing over her with a smug look on his face; she felt a searing pain in her side. She looked down to see that Ariel had driven his foot into her ribs. She began to cough up blood, but he kept kicking her. Ariel crouched in front of her, grabbed a fistful of her hair and brought her face to his.

"Oh Isobel, if only you hadn't done that then I wouldn't have to hurt you." Isobel smirked and spit blood in his face. Ariel snarled in anger and slammed her head into the ground. Ariel stood and noticed that the other three

Manalourins were staring past him. He turned to see Drakonis standing in the middle of the army of defeated rodents. His eyes were dragon like and filled with rage, but

Ariel didn't seem to be bothered. He snapped his fingers and more mutated rodents appeared everywhere. Ariel threw Isobel over his shoulder and carried her as he began to walk toward Drakonis with the others in tow. Ariel stood a good bit away from Drakonis.

"What will you do now? You're alone and surrounded by my army." Drakonis looked around him and realized that he was indeed surrounded, but he turned back to Ariel. "I'm actually grateful that you knocked them both out. They've come so far in their training; they are prodigies that come around every decade or so. However, I'm a prodigy that appears every one hundred years. I didn't want them to think that their training was for nothing, but you're about to find out why I'm considered one of the strongest beings on the planet." They all heard the sound of rings hitting the floor. And before they could even blink Drakonis disappeared and then reappeared in the same spot. When he did, he had both Isobel and Chase in his arms along with all of their weapons. Drakonis put his hand up and surrounded himself with a golden shield.

"I shall drown you in depths of a fiery sea. Chaotic Flame!" A giant golden seal appeared beneath everyone's feet and suddenly it exploded into flames that incinerated everything in the chasm. When the flames died down, Drakonis looked around to see dead bodies littering the ground. He looked up to see that he had created a hole in the roof, so he used his newfound speed to run up the walls and jump out of the hole. He looked around to see that it was nighttime and that he was nowhere near the city. Using his dragon eye, he was able to find it. He put Chase on his back and held Isobel bridal style as he began his long trek back to the city. Drakonis arrived back to his room a few hours before dawn. He decided to drop Chase off first just because he was heavier. He made his way out of Chase's room and into his where he gently placed Isobel on the bed. Drakonis frowned as Isobel started to cough up blood, so he formed a golden ball of mana and put it inside of Isobel. He watched as she was quickly starting to heal. He got up to walk away only to be pulled back by Isobel. Isobel rubbed her eyes sleepily. "Can you help me take my armor off?" Drakonis nodded and helped her remove her armor and placed it on a mannequin. He searched through her drawers to find pajamas for her to wear. He then laid her back down, but she didn't let go of his arm. "Drakonis, don't leave, stay here."

He sighed, "Isobel, I would like to sleep too; I'm kind of tired." Isobel still didn't let go. "You can sleep in here with me; just take your armor off."

"Isobel," he was about to tell her how crazy that sounded.

"Please Drakonis, I don't want to be alone." Drakonis was about to say something when he saw Isobel looking him dead in the eye, so he knew that he wasn't going to win this battle. A little while later, Drakonis climbed into bed wearing shorts and a t-shirt.

"Goodnight, Isobel."

"Goodnight, Drakonis." The duo drifted off into a deep sleep not caring what tomorrow would bring.

Chapter 11
Two Days until the Crucible

Isobel stirred from her sleep, and she felt a warmth that she had never felt before. She lifted her head to meet the sleeping form of Drakonis next to her. She smiled to herself; he looked so peaceful in his sleep. She heard a faint groaning noise, it was Drakonis waking up. She giggled.

"Good morning, sleepy head." He just looked at her, and then turned over to lay on his stomach. Isobel stood up and made her way to the bathroom, but a certain voice in her head stopped her in her tracks. "Hello Isobel, remember me?" It was Rajani. She looked down to see the sword was still attached to her. "I'd hate for you to forget our deal. I will test you later, but first I need dark mana." Isobel thought for a moment about where she was going to get the dark mana. She turned back to the bed and saw that Drakonis was still asleep. Hopefully he could fill the sword with dark mana.

Isobel walked over and poked Drakonis. "Drakonis, wake up." He didn't budge. So she tried a couple of more times before finally giving up, but she smiled as an evil idea came to mind. Isobel climbed on the bed and sat on

Drakonis' back. She sat there for a little while until finally Drakonis turned his head, so he could look at her out of the corner of his eye.

"Excuse me Isobel, but you cannot sit on my back. It hurts from carrying you and Chase all night." Isobel shifted her weight, so that she wasn't on his back but she was still sitting on him. Drakonis groaned. "What is it you want?"

Isobel chuckled "Rajani said she wants dark mana, so will you give her some of yours?" Drakonis grabbed the sword, and he instantly felt a large chunk of his dark mana disappear.

The sword unwrapped itself from around Isobel's arm and fell to the floor. Drakonis was trying to drift back to sleep until he felt a pair of soft hands on his back. He looked back at Isobel; she smiled at him while continuing to massage his back. Drakonis felt all the knots in his back disappear under her touch. But suddenly the door busted open, Isobel and Drakonis turned to see Chase, King Maj and Cyarah standing in the door.

King Maj coughed. "I do hope we aren't interrupting anything."

Drakonis smirked. "Yea, we were just getting to the best part, right Isobel?" Chase's face reddened. Isobel leaned in and whispered into Drakonis' ear. "I'm not sure if you're ready for that, dragon boy." The way she said it ignited a fire in his dragon's blood. Before Isobel could stop him, Drakonis had pinned her.

"Don't wake the dragon if you can't put up a good fight." Drakonis heard the faint sound of electricity, and he turned to see Chase in front of him with a fist full of lightning. Chase swung at Drakonis, but he was surprised when Drakonis wasn't in the same spot anymore. He felt a blade on his neck, and he saw Drakonis smirking at him with Rajani in his hand. Drakonis was smirking at Chase, but then he felt a searing pain in his hand. He looked down to see that the spikes from the handle of the sword were sticking into his hand. Everyone else was shocked as blood protruded from the wounds. Drakonis attempted to let go of the sword, but the spikes were still stuck in his hand. Chase tried to touch the sword, but as soon as he put his hands toward the sword it tried to impale his hand.

"Rajani, would you like to clue me in on why you're impaling me?" He heard her voice in his.

"You aren't my wielder; the girl is, now release me!"

The sword fell from Drakonis' hand and landed on the floor. Isobel grabbed his hand and began to heal him.

"What was that about?" she said examining his hand. Drakonis ran his other hand through his hair.

"Apparently, you're her new wielder, and she didn't take too kindly to me picking her up." "That's impossible." King Maj said. "She can't wield both swords. Isobel, try to pick up Rohaz." Isobel nodded. She attempted to pick up the sword only for her hand to burst into flames as soon as she touched her handle.

"Rohaz, what's the meaning of this!" She screamed in pain, she heard his voice in her head. "You've abandoned me for Rajani, so now I reject you as my wielder, be gone!" Isobel dropped Rohaz just as Drakonis did Rajani. Drakonis grabbed her hand and concealed it within his own. When he opened her hand, he saw that she had some burn marks. But just as he had done before, Drakonis healed her.

Isobel eyed the swords warily. "Does this mean that we have to go through tests again?" King Maj looked thoughtful, "Probably. It's the sword's choice, Isobel. Why don't you do yours, first?" Isobel felt kind of apprehensive about it, but she decided that she had nothing to lose. Drakonis stopped her, before she could pick up the sword,

"How about we get dressed first?" Isobel laughed, "Yeah that would be a good idea. So everyone who's not Drakonis, get out." Everyone looked at each other oddly, but began to walk out of the room. Even Drakonis tried, but Isobel grabbed him by the ear and pulled him back inside.

"Drakonis, did you forget that your armor is in here?" Drakonis mentally smacked himself. Of course he had forgotten that his armor was in there. Isobel smiled knowing she was right.

"I'll take my shower first, then you." She turned to get some clothes. But when she turned back around, she wasn't surprised to see that Drakonis and his armor were gone. She laughed. Drakonis talked a good game, but sometimes he was a baby. Sometime later, Isobel emerged from her room to see the waiting forms of King Maj, Chase, Cyarah and Drakonis.

"Come on. Let's get this over with," she said motioning for them to come into her room. Everyone had gathered around the swords. "Remember Isobel and Drakonis, the swords can only produce illusions in your mind," King Maj said patting his beard. Isobel nodded and picked up Rajani, and everything in the room disappeared. Isobel found herself compressed in complete darkness. She looked around and could barely see as something walked towards her.

"Are you Rajani?" She asked through squinted eyes. The creature was deformed and had bugs crawling out of its body. She tried to run, but she was being held in place by some creatures that were coming out of the ground. She fell to the ground as the creature jumped on her, and she felt more hands coming from the ground to try and pull her down. She tried to struggle, but the creature in her face roared causing saliva to get all over her face. Isobel was mortified when she felt something move on her face. She looked down to see that bugs had come out of the creature's mouth. She screamed in pain as the insects began to burrow into her skin. She looked up and saw that the bugs were the least of her problems. The creature ran its tongue along her face.

"No," she said as the creature opened its mouth to show Isobel all of its sharp teeth and all of the bugs that were crawling around inside. Isobel tried to use her magic, but it didn't work here. The creature leaned in as if to swallow her head whole. There were tears in Isobel's eyes.

"Please, don't do this!" Isobel's screams filled the dark void. Outside of the sword, everyone watched Isobel's face contort as if she were in pain. Suddenly the sword wrapped itself around Isobel's arm. Dark mana was pouring out of the sword, and it began to cover Isobel's body.

King Maj began to panic. "No, something's wrong. Isobel hasn't passed her trial, so the sword is trying to take over her body!"

Chase went wide eyed. "Is there something we can do?"

King Maj shook his head. "No, if we touch the sword then who knows what it would do to us? It could corrupt Isobel, and then we would be easy pickings." Drakonis ignored King Maj's warning. He walked up to Isobel and crouched in front of her. He reached out and touched the sword, and it immediately impaled his hand but he didn't care. As soon as he made contact with the sword, he was pulled into the dark world that was the sword. Drakonis looked around only to find darkness, but then he was met by the same creature that tackled Isobel. Drakonis rolled back to get his bearings. The creature walked up to Drakonis and looked him in the eye, but it growled and turned away.

Isobel's test was a lot different from his. He attempted to attack the creature, but then noticed that he couldn't use any of his powers. So, he did the next best thing; he ran past it.

He noticed that the creature wasn't fast, but it had a lot of reach. As he ran through the darkness, he heard a faint sniffling sound. He followed the sound. And he wasn't surprised that he had found Isobel, but he was surprised at her predicament. She was in a web that was covered in blood, scars and saliva.

"Isobel." he said softly pulling her down. "Drakonis." she said with a pain filled voice. "I'm sorry, I failed. It hurt more than anything else I've been through." When she looked at him, he could see where bugs had dug into her face; he gently pulled each one out. "I know I look hideous, don't I?" Isobel said while chuckling. Drakonis brought her closer to him. "I don't care how you look, I just want you to be safe." Isobel snuggled herself into his chest, and she saw the faint blush on his face.

"What's wrong Drakonis? where's all that talk about waking the dragon?" She said smiling slyly.

Drakonis grimaced. "I don't think this the right situation…"

Isobel interrupted him, "Oh, just shut up and kiss me." Before Drakonis could say anything, Isobel threw her arms around his neck and brought him into a kiss. To say it was unexpected was an understatement. After what felt like an eternity, they separated. Drakonis felt Isobel hit him in the chest, so he looked at her and raised a brow.

"What was that for?" He saw her smile like never before; it was so golden and full of life. "Because the guy is supposed to make the first move not the girl. And you weren't going to do it, so I had to." Drakonis rolled his eyes. "Whatever." Isobel snuggled back into his chest when she looked back up to see the same creature that tormented her standing behind them. She froze; Drakonis followed her gaze to see the creature standing behind them. It just stared at them, but then pointed to Isobel with one of its disgusting fingers. Drakonis looked back at Isobel.

"It's your trial, and you have to finish it."

Isobel shook her head. "I don't know what to do and last time it almost…" she trailed off looking back to where Drakonis had found her.

"Don't let it corrupt your golden soul; that's your trial." Drakonis kissed her forehead and smiled. Isobel looked between the creature and Drakonis then nodded. Isobel stood and walked in front of the creature. She looked it in the eye and watched in disgust as its skin started to contort. The creatures began to transform, and the darkness around them began to give shape and turn into something

165

that dwelled deep within the heart of Isobel. In front of them stood the creature that left a scar on not only Isobel, but the entire world. Here was the dragon of darkness. The dragon let out a menacing laugh that terrified Isobel to her core. Isobel felt something grasp her hand, and saw Drakonis standing next to her with his hand in hers. "Come on, Isobel" he said smiling. "Let's get through this and go home." Isobel nodded and faced the creature that haunted her dreams. The dragon stood, reared its head back and released a torrent of black flames burning everything around the people in front of it, but the fire did not touch the two. The dragon looked at the two and laughed once more "We shall meet again Isobel, but your savior won't be able to save you." Then the creature dissipated and light was brought to the darkness.

"You've passed my test with a little bit of help from the outside, and I'll allow it since Drakonis does provide me with dark mana. I accept you as my new wielder." With that said, they were thrust back into the real world. They turned to see King Maj, Cyarah and Chase staring at them. Isobel snickered. "I guess they want to know what happened." They all nodded. Drakonis had a thoughtful expression on his face.

"Our tests were completely different. When I did mine, I had to subjugate the souls of the damned. Isobel had to stand up to this creature, but I don't know why."

"My test was for me to face my fears, but I failed the first time until you came into the sword."

"How about we agree not to talk about what happened in there?" She said with a faint blush, and he nodded in agreement. Drakonis sighed, "Alright, let's get this over with." Drakonis sat on the ground, and held Rohaz. He was immediately pulled into whatever the sword had planned for him. He opened his eyes to see a vast luscious field of grass and the sun bearing down on himself. He felt at peace, but he was then hit in the face with a ball. Drakonis looked around; battle ready, but he then noticed the tall figure in front of him.

"Come on, Drakonis, you said you wanted to play catch." Drakonis narrowed his eyes at the man. "Who are you?" He said apprehensively. The man was surprised as he began walking towards Drakonis.

"Did that ball hit you too hard?" Drakonis pulled out his sword and pointed it at the man, "Don't make me repeat myself."

The man burst out laughing. "Son, what are you going to do with a wooden sword?" Drakonis didn't even notice it was a wooden sword, so he looked at himself again and noticed something that made him speechless. "I'm...I'm... I'm a kid!" The man was now worried about Drakonis.

"Come on, Koni, let's get you home."

Drakonis froze. "Only my father calls me that."

The man was really confused. "Uh, yea, I am your dad."

Drakonis shook his head. "No, this is all an illusion caused by Rohaz."

The man broke out into full blown laughter. "That wooden sword of yours creates illusions; that's a new one.

Come on. Let's get home before your mother fries us both." The man picked up Drakonis and began walking toward his home. Drakonis was in deep thought, but he just knew this was an illusion. They arrived at a large town bustling with people. As they came to a stop, Drakonis marveled at how large the house was. The house itself was tall with large windows that added to the overall style of the home He felt like he was home. The man opened the door allowing Drakonis to see how beautiful the house was on the inside. Drakonis looked around the home and it was even larger on the inside. The home gave off a snug and comfortable feeling, It felt welcoming . Drakonis didn't miss the large purplish mass that moved as soon as they walked in. Drakonis jumped back as the mass moved toward them.

When Drakonis could finally make out what the creature was, he was beyond shocked. "Azzaria, stop scaring the poor boy." The man said scolding the very large dragon. The dragon nuzzled her face against the man. "Adel; he is our son, so he doesn't get scared." Drakonis watched the interactions between the two, and thought, 'no, this wasn't real,' and it couldn't be real. The dragon must have noticed his turmoil. "What's wrong Drakonis?" She said wrapping her arms around him. Drakonis pushed away from her.

"No, this isn't real! This isn't real!" He screamed looking at his parents. "This can't be real, because you're dead." He said pointing at his father, and then to his mother. "You...you hate me, because I look like dad. You hate me, because I'm not the full blooded dragon you wanted. You hate me, because I wasn't strong enough to save dad. You pawned me off on D'Merrion to do with me as he saw fit.

You didn't even come around to check up on me!" Tears were streaming down Drakonis' face. "You never cared about me. You hated me over things that I couldn't control, and you sacrificed my soul to free D'Merrion. What loving parent would do that?" Drakonis was sobbing uncontrollably. "It's not fair! It's not fair! I never had a family growing up. I was always celebrating my birthdays alone. The only people I ever had were grandpa and King Maj. What parent throws their child away like trash? All I wanted to do was make you both proud of me. Especially you, mom because you're still alive, but nothing I did would ever be enough for you. What did I do to deserve such hate?!

Tell me what I did, so I can fix it and have my mother back!" Everything was silent. then Drakonis felt his parents embrace after his little episode.

"Drakonis," his mother said softly. "I am so sorry, I'm sorry that you feel that way, and I'm sorry that you had to spend so many birthdays without your father and me. I'm sorry that I've been a terrible mother all my life. You're the most amazing child anyone could ask for even if you're a half blood. I will always love you my little halfling." She nuzzled her face against his; wiping the tears on his face. Drakonis smiled through his teary eyes, but then frowned.

"It doesn't matter because all of this is an illusion, and I'll have to leave eventually."

Adel smiled. "You don't have to leave if you don't want to; you can stay here with us." Drakonis' face brightened up at the thought of staying with his parents, but he then remembered his responsibilities in the real world. Drakonis watched Adel walk and then come back with something in his hand. Azzaria and Adel both had huge grins on their face.

"Happy Birthday!" They said in unison while holding a birthday cake. Drakonis ran up and hugged his parents. "I never want to leave." He said through tears of joy. He didn't care what was happening in the real world. He'd take this illusion over the real world any day of the week. Outside of the illusion, the group was watching Drakonis to see if anything was happening. Isobel and King Maj were the only ones who seemed worried. Chase then spoke up, "Come on, guys, it's Drakonis! I'm sure he's fine."

Isobel shook her head. "When I was being tested, I didn't take this long." Everyone was startled when Drakonis' hand burst into flames, and the fire was slowly moving up his arm. Everyone jumped into action to try and put out the flames.

Chase ran and grabbed a fire extinguisher. "Stand back everyone!" He shouted. He sprayed the fire, but it didn't diminish in the slightest. "It's the same thing that happened with Isobel; he isn't passing the trial so the sword is trying to consume him." To say that everyone was shocked was an understatement. Isobel ran and sat down in front of Drakonis. She cast a quick spell and then put her hands on the sword but as soon as she did her hand burst into fire. She didn't feel it at first thanks to the spell, but she had a limited amount of time before it would wear off. Isobel was pulled into the sword much like before, but this time she saw a place that she had never been before. It was a fairly large town in her opinion. She kept walking through the town until she saw a dragon fly over. "Could that be Drakonis?" she quickly began to follow the dragon. When it finally landed, she noticed people on its back. One was a little boy and another a grown man. She hid behind a tree, and continued to watch the group in front of her. They looked and acted like a family. Isobel mentally smacked herself. It was Drakonis' family. She barely ducked when the dragon's claws cut the tree in half.

The dragon glared angrily at her. "Are you one of those divine knights here to kill me and my family?" Isobel quickly shook her head

"No, I'm a friend of Drakonis."

"Isobel, what are you doing here?" said Drakonis with surprise.

"Drakonis, Rohaz is trying to consume you, so I came here to help you. You have to break the illusion or else you'll die."

Drakonis shook his head. "I don't care, I like this illusion! I like having my family here. I don't care. I would give up anything to stay."

Isobel was very surprised by what Drakonis was saying. "What about all of your friends? What about the kids? What about your grandfather? What about me?" She said, whispering the last part.

"I don't care. I finally have my own family, my own childhood without all those hardships, and I won't give it up so I suggest you leave." Isobel was about to walk toward Drakonis until Azzaria stopped her. "He said leave, so you can go willingly or I can make you go."

Isobel glared at Azzaria. "I guess you'll have to make me." Azzaria stood on her hind legs and took in a giant breath. As soon as she released it, she let loose a wave of fire larger than Isobel had ever seen. The fire burned down the forest and everything in it. Isobel had shielded herself, but the fire was too much and broke through the shield giving her burns on parts of her body. Azzaria stood over Isobel prepared to finish her off. Isobel was laying on the ground looking up at the dragon.

"If you're really Drakonis' parents and you actually love him, then you'd free him because if you don't then he will die and no parent wants that." This caused Azzaria to stop. She looked back to where Adel and Drakonis stood.

She proceeded to walk over to them. "Drakonis," she said bringing her head down to him, "Your father and I love you, but we won't risk your life to be with you, right, Adel?" Adel had to agree. They loved Drakonis too much to let him die.

Drakonis shook his head. "No, I don't care if I die. I just want to be with you guys. I don't have anyone else."

Adel let out a sad chuckle. "You have all of your friends from the real world, and you have her." He pointed at Isobel who was standing not too far from them. "She came all this way to help you, and even stood up to your mother for you. That's a dedication that your mother and I would approve of."

Drakonis began to tear up. "I don't want to go."

Azzaria brought Drakonis and Adel into a hug. "I know you don't want to, but you have to. Go and be a man that we would be proud to call our son. Show the world that you're proud of your heritage and protect those closest to you, because they will always be there for you." Isobel had never seen Drakonis cry and it broke her heart, because no one should have to go through what he had gone through. Sadly, the world wasn't as nice as this one.

Azzaria and Adel turned to Isobel. "Take care of our son. You're the type of girl we'd approve of him being with for the rest of his life."

Isobel blushed and nodded. The parents turned back to their son, "It's time to go, Drakonis. Just remember; even in your darkest hour, we love you." Drakonis smiled.

"I love you too, mom and dad. And I always will." Drakonis went and stood next to Isobel. He turned to look at his parents one last time, before he let out a large burst of mana that shattered the illusion completely. Drakonis opened his eyes and looked around; he immediately felt a burning sensation in his arm. He took his arm gauntlet off to see that he had mild burns on his arm. He looked up to see Isobel sitting in front of him with her hand on his. As gently as he could, he took her armor off her hand. She also had burn marks, but hers were on her hand and a lot more severe than his. He held her hand in his and began to heal them both. Isobel watched Drakonis heal her hand; his facial expression was unreadable. She knew that he was hurting on the inside, but who wouldn't be? He had the perfect life inside of the illusion, and he had to throw it all away.

Drakonis stood up after healing Isobel. King Maj, what did you need?"

King Maj could hear the lifelessness in Drakonis' voice. "I was actually ordered to come see if you retrieved the crown."

Drakonis face palmed. He had completely forgotten about the crown.

"I honestly think that I destroyed it. I used my dragon spell and destroyed everything." Another voice entered the room. "It's a shame about my crown, but to hear Drakonis embracing his heritage brings joy to my old heart."

Everyone turned to see D'Merrion standing in the doorway. They all bowed.

"Lord D'Merrion," everyone said in unison. He ignored them.

"Drakonis, I see you haven't been slacking on your training, so I've come with a proposal to get you back into my good graces. I want you to join the crucible with Chase, and fight against the two fighters whom I chose."

Drakonis could see that something was off. "I'm grateful that you'd offer me this position father, but what about the rule system that you put in place?"

D'Merrion grinned. "That's an excellent question. I've decided on a seven day event with two rounds a day. I already have the names of the participants." King D'Merrion showed no emotion in his face, so Drakonis couldn't see if there was any more information he was hiding.

"I'd be honored to be a part of it."

The king nodded and proceeded to leave the room, but then stopped. "King Maj, I would expect you to have a new crown made for me by the time the crucible begins." With that said, he left the room.

Chase had a thoughtful expression. "After everything that's been happening, I completely forgot about the crucible. When is the start date?"

Drakonis stood and walked over to the nearest calendar. He sighed and hit his head against the wall. "The crucible begins tomorrow."

No one in the room could believe it. Chase shook his head, "There's no way it could be that soon. We haven't been training for that long unless the gods got together and decided to speed up time."

Cyarah rolled her eyes. "Even if it is in two days, I feel that Chase is ready for whatever D'Merrion can throw at him."

Drakonis agreed. "King Maj, do you think you could get more of those inhibitor rings?" King Maj nodded. "Yea, what do you need them for?"

Drakonis sighed. "I lost mine, and I need to give some to Chase to replace the clothes because he can quickly take the rings off in case of emergencies. Also Chase, I've been wanting to ask this, but you can't use magic through spells can you?"

Chase rubbed his head as he laughed nervously. "No, I channel my magic throughout my body and it manifests lightning which increases my speed and my strength."

This peaked Cyarah's interest. "Have you ever tried to force it outside of your body in a condensed form?"

Chase shook his head. "Never really thought about trying it. Do you think you could show me how?"

Cyarah was taken aback, she really thought he hated her. "I...sure, I'd be happy to, but only if it's okay with Drakonis."

Everyone looked at Drakonis to see what he'd say. "I'd be grateful if you did, but don't forget the sentinels are attracted to magic so you might have to go outside the city walls." They both nodded and made their way to the door.

King Maj met them there. "Before you leave for the city walls, you should come and get the inhibitor rings." After they left the room, only Isobel and Drakonis were left. Isobel turned to Drakonis.

"So, what are we going to do today?"

Drakonis turned away from her. "I don't know nor do

I care. You can do what you want." Isobel frowned. "Drakonis, I'm sorry, but I had to wake you from the illusion." Drakonis just growled and began to walk away.

"Drakonis, drop the tough guy act. I know it hurts, but you don't have to bottle it up inside." He ignored her and kept walking, but she had had enough. "Drakonis, stop being such a coward!" That stopped him in his tracks. She continued, "You lost your family once before, so why should it bother you that you lost them again?"

Now Drakonis had had enough. "What would you know about losing your whole family, you spoiled little brat? You couldn't comprehend how I felt, because you've had everything handed to you on a silver platter. So tell me, tell me how you know anything about how I feel, and what I'm going through."

They were face to face with waves of anger rolling from Drakonis, but Isobel did the unthinkable. She wrapped her arms around Drakonis, and brought him into a hug. Her voice was angelic, "I won't know or understand Drakonis unless you tell me." Drakonis hated it, but there was something about Isobel that angered and calmed him. Isobel watched Drakonis detach himself from her and sit down on a sofa. Isobel sat next to him, and she was surprised when Drakonis laid his head on her lap. She smiled a little and began to run her hand through his hair. The deep rumbling in his chest told her that his dragon half really enjoyed it.

"Drakonis, do you want to talk to me about it?" Drakonis didn't respond. "It's okay if you don't want to, but I'll be here if you do." Drakonis closed his eyes enjoying the feeling of her hand through his hair. "Drakonis, you may not know it, but you mean a lot to a lot of people." Isobel looked down to see Drakonis fast asleep. She frowned then grinned as she leaned into his ear and said, "So, Koni, what do you have planned for today?"

His eyes shot open. "One, don't ever call me that again. Two, I plan on sleeping all day." "Koni, Koni, Koni, I don't want to be in this room all day." She huffed.

He rolled his eyes at her. "You should have gone with Chase and Cyarah."

Isobel scoffed, "But I wouldn't have been able to spend time with my dragon prince." The words had escaped her lips, before she could cover her mouth.

Drakonis looked up at her and smirked. "Your dragon prince?" He asked questionably. Isobel had a light blush on her cheeks. "Well, you know, since I'm a spoiled brat and get everything I want handed to me, I think I want a dragon prince."

Drakonis' voice softened. "I apologize for what I said."

Isobel pecked Drakonis on the nose. "It's okay, I shouldn't have provoked you. Come on, let's go back to bed. I can't imagine how laying on my legs while I have armor on can be comfortable for you." Drakonis stood and began to walk to his room with Isobel in tow. Drakonis took off his armor and put it back on the mannequin, then he laid down in his bed and closed his eyes. He felt shuffling next him, he ignored it but then he couldn't ignore her hand drawing circles on his back.

He sighed. "Isobel, what are you doing?"

She giggled, "Just drawing the place where your wings are going to come out."

He turned toward her. She was beautiful, although he wouldn't tell her that.

"Half breed dragons don't have wings." he stated.

She frowned slightly. How do you know that?"

He just rolled his eyes. "Because I've never heard of it."

"Well, I've never heard of a dragon hybrid until now. So just because we haven't seen it, doesn't make it not exist."

She stared at Drakonis never noticing how enticing his eyes were. "Drakonis, your eyes are like mine color wise."

He shook his head. "No, you have gold eyes. I have amber eyes, but I guess you could say they're in the same family. I wouldn't know; I'm not an artist."

Isobel thought about something. "Hey, Drakonis, use your dragon eyes." He just looked at her, but she watched as his normal amber eyes transitioned into reptile eyes.

"It looks like you're staring into my soul," said Isobel.

When he looked at her with his normal eyes they gave off a caring feeling, but when he looked at her with his dragon eyes, it looked as if he was stalking his prey. He turned his eyes back into his normal ones.

"Well, you're right. When I have my dragon eyes, I can see people's souls and a bunch of other things."

Drakonis laid there for a moment thinking. "Isobel, what is your connection with the dragon of darkness?" Isobel hesitated for a moment before a sad smile and said, "Nothing good. When I was younger, the dragon attacked my home; it killed everyone except me. And to this day, I don't know why. The dragon toyed with me allowing me to run, but then caught me, it was like a game of cat and mouse to him. After holding me hostage, he let me go but not before placing this Mark on my neck. He said that once the mark is done corrupting my soul and driving me mad, then he would come back and put me out of my misery. The only way for me to remove the mark is to kill him, but that's easier said than done. That's why I stayed here. I was hoping that you could lead me to him; however, that's not the case anymore."

Isobel turned to see Drakonis dozing off, but she could only laugh to herself. She was glad he fell asleep because her story didn't sound believable. She wondered how Chase was doing; he always had problems when it came to magic. She herself began to drift off into the void. She could go for more sleep. The gods knew she needed it.

Chapter 12
One day until the Crucible

Chase and Cyarah were following King Maj to the Forge. The walk was silent and a little awkward. King Maj looked out of the corner of his eye at the two people behind him. Cyarah had a straight face, but you could tell that she was deep in thought. Chase; however, wore his emotions on his face. He was deep in thought. These two were really odd, but King Maj could only guess that Chase had feelings for this ice queen. She; on the other hand, only had feelings for science. When they finally arrived at the forge, he told the two to wait outside. He quickly fetched the inhibitor rings, and brought them out to Chase.

"Alright Chase. You can wear five at one time, but your body wouldn't be able to handle any more than that. The rings work differently than the clothes Drakonis had you wear. They restrict your body's movements to a certain degree. For example, if you were to jump with these on, you won't go as high as you normally would. When you finally get used to them and take them off, you're going to feel like a new man." Chase put the rings on and instantly felt their effects.

Cyarah watched Chase's sluggish movements and said, "Thank you, King Maj. I shall take it from here." The king nodded and waved the duo off. Thanks to the effects of the rings, Chase was struggling to keep up with Cyarah, and she was walking very slowly.

"So Cyarah, why did you agree to help me?"

She didn't make eye contact as she spoke. "Because I feel indebted to you, Drakonis and Isobel. However; they don't need my help with anything right now, but you do."

Chase saw that they were coming up on the city walls but

Cyarah continued, "It's my turn to ask you a question Chase. Your magic is different from Isobel's. She uses spells, but you channel your magic through your body. Why is that?"

Chase sighed. "Every one of the knights are different. Isobel was the favorite, because she was the only one to inherit every type of magic from our predecessors. As for my magic; when I got mine, it was corrupted so I wasn't able to use spells. I could only use lightning to increase my speed and strength."

Cyarah was absorbing everything he was saying.

"How do you adopt the powers of your predecessors?" She looked back at Chase, but his facial expression told her that he wasn't going to answer so she said, "You always seem to get the short end of the stick, don't you?"

She heard his faint chuckle. "Yea, you can blame that on my creator." They passed the gates of the city and entered the lush lands outside of the walls.

Cyarah stopped. "Since we are basically free of the guardians, I guess we can cut loose." She looked at Chase and smiled; the twinkle in her eyes made him nervous. "See if you can keep up!" Chase's jaw hung open at the sight, but then he started to grin. He may not win against her, but he wasn't going to lose too badly. He charged himself with lightning and took off after her. After a while, Chase had finally caught up to Cyarah. She looked back to see a yellow bolt catching up to her, and she smiled to herself. Chase was an interesting creature; more so than others. She slid to a halt with Chase right behind her.

Chase looked around and saw that they were in the ruins of a suburban area. "What are we doing here, Cyarah?"

She grinned slightly at him. "We are here to cut loose." Cyarah began to crack her knuckles and released her power. Chase had to take a step back at the sheer amount of dark mana radiating from Cyarah. He watched as she slammed both hands into the ground, and two wolf like creatures made of pure dark mana were raised from the ground. He watched in awe as they both circled Cyarah in a protective fashion.

"Your type of magic is similar to dark mana, but right now you'd probably only be able to make small things. Eventually, you'll be able to create almost anything your mind can think of." Cyarah closed her eyes and concentrated for a moment; the two wolves collided into each other to form something else. An exact replica of Drakonis stood next to Cyarah.

Chase whistled. "Not bad, but you seem to be missing one important thing."

Cyarah scoffed. "Enlighten me?" Chase dashed toward the copy and punched him causing him to explode into dark mana. Chase was startled when the mana wrapped itself around him and began to squeeze his body. Chase quickly used his power to his advantage. Turning himself into a lightning bolt, he quickly escaped the confines of his entrapment. Cyarah waved her hand causing the dark mana to dissipate into nothing. She sat down then motioned for

Chase to sit across from her. "Molding your mana like I did takes a high level of concentration. The thing is, you already know how to mold because you mold your body into lightning to move fast. It's the same concept, except you have to mold it outside of your body and use your imagination to give it form. Let's start off with something small for now. I want you to make a ball of lightning in your hand." Chase sat across from her and started concentrating. Some time had passed, and Chase was still trying to create a ball of lighting in his hands. Cyarah could see that he was struggling, so she cupped his hands in hers.

"Chase, stop before you pop a blood vessel. How did you first learn how to use your magic?" Chase thought for a moment. "It usually just comes to me when I really need it. When all of the knights inherited their powers, everyone turned their back on me; except Isobel. She refused to. She was there for me, even when I was disowned." Chase let out a soft chuckle. "One day, we were playing, and then they came and told Isobel she couldn't play anymore because she had to train. They said that they were going to kill me, so that they could have my power sent to someone else and that they hoped the transfer wouldn't mess up. They had the other knights hold me and Isobel. She struggled, but I didn't. I just wanted all of the hate and malice to end. Then one of the divines struck Isobel, and I felt so enraged. How dare they hit my best friend? She was like a sister to me. All of a sudden, I was covered in lightning, and I attacked everyone. The only person who was safe was Isobel. I knocked all the knights out and then went after the divines, but they instantly knocked me out. Long story short, they decided to keep me alive to be Isobel's guardian." Cyarah was absorbing everything that Chase was saying. She had more questions about his story, but she'd save that for later.

When he finished, she stood up. "I have an idea that you probably won't like, but you only need to do one thing for me." Cyarah's voice was as cold as ice, and her stare could melt fire.

Chase gulped. "What do you need me to do?" The dread in his voice was evident. She uttered one word before everything turned into a nightmare. "Survive."

Chase was sitting inside one of the abandoned Houses. He was a little hurt, but his ego was the only thing that was really bruised. Cyarah was going all out on him, and he couldn't believe that she was this strong. It hurt him to know that she always held back against him. Even with his lightning mana coursing through his body, he could

barely dodge hers. He quickly jumped out the window as a
fist collided with the building which caused it to collapse.
He barely had time to catch his breath, before Cyarah was
on him again. Her fist collided with his causing a shock
wave. They began to trade blows, and Chase knew he had
to become serious. He dodged Cyarah's next blow,
delivered a kick to her side then followed up with an elbow
to her jaw. Cyarah stumbled back then glared at Chase. She
noticed that the goofy smile on his face was gone, and it was
now replaced with a serious look. He had a fire in his eyes;
a desire to live. They clashed once again trading blows.
Cyarah knew if she wanted to help him, then she would
need to step it up. Cyarah tried to get some distance from
Chase, but he wouldn't let up. It was an admirable quality,
but there comes a time when you have to reevaluate your
strategy. Cyarah formed a condensed ball of dark mana,
and slammed it into Chase sending him flying. Cyarah
wasted no time and began to chant something dark. Black
markings began to cover her body, and her hair and eyes
turned black. She dashed toward Chase and turned the even
fight into a one sided beat down. He was now her new
punching bag. Chase was surprised by what Cyarah had
done. She used her dark mana to increase her speed,
strength and durability. Chase refused to lose; even after it

was evident that he was going to. He watched as Cyarah brought her hands together and began to chant something. Her dark mana began to form something huge behind her. Huge could not fully describe the creature that stood behind her. "Witness the embodiment of dark mana; the Dark Elemental. You should feel honored Chase, you're the second person I've ever used this on." The creature stepped where Chase was, but he was able to dodge. Chase used his lighting and began to deliver blows to the titan, but nothing was harming it. The creature swatted Chase away sending him flying. Chase was attempting to stand, but couldn't find the strength to do so.

"Come on, Chase. Get up. I know you can do it." Chase was barely conscious. A yell stopped him as he looked up to see the titan holding Cyarah in its giant hand.

It spoke in its deep booming voice. "I told you before never to summon me again. You broke our contract, manipulated my power and harmed my people. It is time for you to pay!" The creature began to squeeze her body, but frowned when she didn't scream.

"You know it's going to take a lot more than that to even make me shed a tear."

The creature smirked. "You talk a big game, but all that dark mana you have belongs to me. The creature began to absorb all of the dark mana that Cyarah had. Chase knew that she would die if she had all of it taken away. The titan began to apply more pressure to Cyarah's body while draining her of her mana. Cyarah bit her tongue, so that she wouldn't give him the satisfaction of hearing her scream in pain. The titan used his other hand to grab one of Cyarah's arms. He began to crush it which actually caused Cyarah to scream. Chase watched, but there was nothing he could do. Suddenly, something caused the creature harm. Cyarah turned to see Lydia biting the hand that was holding her. The titan yelped in annoyance, but he grabbed Lydia while still holding onto Cyarah.

"Impudent creature, do you not know who you've bitten!?" The titan threw Lydia onto the ground and then stomped on her. Chase could hear the sounds of Cyarah crying and begging him to stop, but the creature wouldn't relent.

Chase hated what he was hearing, but then a voice whispered in his ear. "Do you want the power to save them?" Chase didn't need to answer the voice, because it already knew. "I grant you power child; the power to protect those you care for, and the power to smite those who would stand in your way. I; the Lightning Elemental, give you that power." The voice was gone, but Chase felt a new-found power fuel his burning fire. He stood up feeling the power course through his veins. He stuck his hand out and concentrated. But instead of seeing his usual; a ball, it was a bolt- a very large lightning bolt. Chase threw it into the titan which caused a gaping hole in his chest. The titan and Cyarah were both surprised at what happened. The titan fell to its knees finally letting go of Cyarah.

"Who dares?" He roared in pain.

He looked around to see Chase with another bolt in his hand. "I dare! You made Cyarah cry, and for that I'll never forgive you." The creature swiped at Chase only for it to have its arm destroyed. Chase formed a giant bolt even bigger than the others. He ran up to the downed titan, and shoved the bolt into it causing the being to dissipate into nothing. Chase walked toward where Cyarah was lying next to Lydia. "Will she be alright?" Cyarah turned toward him as Lydia said, "Hopefully with the right medical equipment, she might be able to make a full recovery."

Chase smiled his signature smile. "That's good, I'm glad you both are okay."

Chase felt a pair of arms pull him into a hug. "Thank you Chase, I'll never forget this and I'll always be thankful for what you've done." Chase returned the hug, but before he could respond he felt exhaustion and fatigue overcome him. For the first time today, he allowed darkness to overcome him. Cyarah felt Chase's body slump against hers. "Go ahead and sleep, Chase. You earned it; but sadly, this is only the beginning. You made a deal with the Lightning Element, and life's only going to get harder for you from now on."

Chapter 13
Day of the Crucible

Drakonis woke to the sound of a deep rumbling, and sat up in his bed. He looked over to notice that the rumbling noise was coming from Isobel. He was going to hold that against her. He walked to the bathroom to prepare himself for the day. As Drakonis was putting on the last few pieces of his armor, he heard Isobel getting up from the bed.

"Where are you going?" She asked while stretching and yawning. Drakonis looked back at her and laughed; her hair looked ridiculous. Isobel guessing what he was laughing at rushed into the bathroom and closed the door. Drakonis walked out of the bedroom and toward Chase's room. Seeing that the door was still open, Drakonis knew that Chase had not come back to his room last night. Isobel came out of her room wearing her armor.

She peeked in Chase's room to notice that he was missing. "Where do you think he is?" Drakonis thought for a moment. "If I had to guess, I'd say that he's probably in Cyarah's room. Let's head over there to see if he's alright." Drakonis and Isobel left their room and began to make their way throughout the castle. They entered a part of the castle where Isobel had never been before. Everything in here was so technological, and it seemed as if everything that was being studied before D'Merrion was being studied here. Different creatures in lab coats were all working on different things.

Isobel saw some of the weapons that her fellow knights had used. "Drakonis, what are they trying to do here?" Isobel said while pointing at the weapons.

Drakonis stopped and looked. "Honestly, I couldn't tell you. I have no jurisdiction here, and I don't come here too often." Isobel just nodded and continued to follow Drakonis. They came to the end of the hallway and entered the final door. It was Cyarah's personal lab. As they entered the room, two things stood out to the duo. Two large containers sat in the middle of the room. One had Chase in it, and the other housed Lydia. But in front of the containers, was Cyarah sitting in her chair typing something on her computer.

Cyarah looked back at Drakonis and Isobel. "You guys are here earlier than I expected. Well, Chase is about to wake up, so it's good that you are here."

Isobel began to glare at Cyarah. "What happened to Chase, and why is he in that thing?" Cyarah yawned and lazily looked at Isobel. "Well, to answer your first question.

Chase exhausted all of his power yesterday, so he's in there so that he doesn't suffer from mana exhaustion." Everyone watched as Chase's container beeped and then opened.

Chase opened his eyes and took in the room around him. "So guys, how long have I been out?"

Everyone looked at Cyarah. "You've been out for about five hours, and you've been in the pod for three." Chase went wide eyed, "How did we get back to the city?"

Cyarah looked back down at her computer. "I called in a favor from one of the scientists here. Anymore questions, you'd like to ask me?"

Chase nodded, "Where is Lydia?" Cyarah just pointed at the container next to him.

"She will be out of commission for a while; but other than that, she'll make a full recovery." Chase let out a breath that he didn't know he was holding in. "That's good, now how about we get some food because I'm in starving."

Drakonis began to speak. "How about we go out into the city to eat and get everyone measured for their outfits that they will be wearing for the ball after the crucible." To everyone's surprise, Cyarah had agreed to go with them.

The four of them began to make their way through the castle and into the city. As they were walking, Drakonis noticed that as Chase talked to Cyarah, she had actually smiled and even laughed.

"So Chase, what happened yesterday during your training?"

Chase was about to say something, but then his stomach growled. He began to laugh. "How about I tell you after I eat?" They continued to walk throughout the streets when Drakonis finally stopped. They had arrived at a restaurant; it was an all you can eat buffet. As they all seated and got their food, Chase began to explain the events of his training. Throughout his story, Chase decided to leave out the part about the dark and lightning elementals. "So when Cyarah had finally pushed me to the brink of death, I was able to use my mana to its full extent." Drakonis and Isobel absorbed everything Chase was saying, and they were proud of him. He had really stepped up. And this new power of his would allow him to hopefully win the crucible. After paying for their meal, the group made their way back to town. Trumpets began to go off, and people and creatures alike began to flood the streets. There were soldiers marching with flags waving in the air. Isobel and Chase watched in awe. Isobel turned to look at Drakonis, and saw that he had a shocked look on his face which quickly turned to indifference. Walking down the street was a large purple and black dragon with her wings folded around her neck. Behind her were six guards; three on each side wearing all black armor with different weapons. The dragon spotted Drakonis in the crowd, but she made no move to speak to him. The look on her face told them that all they needed to be careful. The rest of the day was uneventful, but the group decided to spend the rest of the day away from the castle. They all knew what the next few days had in store for them.

And if they weren't ready, then they would fail. Drakonis was feeling some type of way. He was hurt to see his mom again, especially after what his sword had put him through.

He felt someone's hand intertwine with his, and he looked to see Isobel giving him a worried stare.

She rubbed his hand with her thumb. "Come on, Koni. I'll be right here by your side through everything."

Drakonis laughed a little. "Are you sure you can handle me?" Isobel's laugh was music to his ears.

"I guess we will have to see, huh?" Chase and Cyarah were walking far behind Drakonis and Isobel.

"Chase." Cyarah said looking away, "I want to thank you for not telling them my secret. I owe you one." Chase smiled a genuine smile. "Well, there's this ball thing that I have to go to, and I would like you to accompany me but in something that isn't a lab coat."

Cyarah rolled her eyes. "Sure, I'll go. But just for that comment, I'm going to wear my lab coat."

They both started to laugh. But as their laughter died down, Cyarah gave Chase one more hug. "Thanks for everything. I'll see you tomorrow at the crucible."

Chase just smiled and waved her off, and then he turned to catch up with the Drakonis and Isobel only to see them both grinning at him. A blush creeped onto Chase's face. "What are you lovebirds looking at?"

As they entered the castle, they all went their separate ways. Sleep was the last thing on everyone's mind, but they knew that they needed it more than anything else. Come tomorrow, everything was going to change. The night went by fast, and then came morning. A banging on the door caused everyone to wake up. Drakonis went to the door to see some of the guards standing on the other side.

His eyes narrowed. "What do you want?"

One of them stepped forward. "We have orders to bring Chase to the crucible."

Drakonis frowned. "I am fully capable of taking him there myself."

The guards reached for their weapons. "We have strict orders to do so by force if we have to." Drakonis growled menacingly causing them to take a step back. He was about to retort, when Chase put his hand on Drakonis' shoulder. "It's fine Drakonis. I'll see you guys in the arena." Drakonis; seeing that Chase was already prepared, didn't have any choice but to let him go with the guards.

Isobel came out and hugged Chase. "We will be rooting you on the whole time." Chase smiled and returned her hug. Isobel and Drakonis watched as Chase was taken away by the guards. Drakonis turned to Isobel. "Come on, let's get dressed so we can be there before it starts." Sometime later, Isobel and Drakonis were running throughout the kingdom to get to the crucible. The streets were very busy, but that didn't stop the duo from getting to the crucible. The building itself was very much like a roman arena except larger and more modern. When they got to the arena, they saw Cyarah standing at the door to get in. And when she saw them, she motioned for them to follow her.

They followed Cyarah throughout the different hallways until they came upon a large locked door with two guards standing in front. Cyarah flashed her badge at them, and they quickly stood aside. As the door opened, they all saw Chase sitting in a room with two doors; one was the door they walked into and the other was the door to the arena.

"Hey guys; took you long enough to get here." Chase teased, smiling. The tension that was built up melted away.

Drakonis was the first to speak. "You don't look nervous for a guy who's about to fight in the most deadly game in the world."

Chase scoffed. "Me? Nervous? Please. More like terrified, but I have enough confidence in my skill and everything I've learned. I can take anyone on." Everyone smiled at his determination, but their conversation was cut short as one of the guards tapped on the door.

"I'm going to have to ask you all to leave; the human is fighting in five minutes." Drakonis saw the look that Chase was giving Cyarah. So after giving Chase some good advice, Drakonis ushered Isobel out of the room leaving only Cyarah and Chase.

Cyarah pulled Chase into a hug. "Don't die on me, Chase; I've yet to experiment on you." Chase just smiled. "Well, how about you give me a reason to live?"

Cyarah rolled her eyes. "You're so cheesy." But before Chase could respond, Cyarah planted a kiss on his lips. It was over in seconds, but it felt like an eternity.

Chase's face turned red, as Cyarah walked out of the door. She looked back at Chase. "I hope that is a good reason to live."

With that the doors closed behind her, Chase finally found the words he wanted to say. "That's definitely a good reason to live." Chase turned and watched the door to the arena open. "Aviance, are you ready for this?"

The construct floated next to him. "As ready as I'll ever be, lover boy." Chase walked through the door only to be blinded by sunlight. After his eyes adjusted, he looked around to see millions of people and creatures in the stands. However, there were only three faces he was looking for, as he looked up to the spectator box, he saw D'Merrion, Addurog and Azzaria but then in another spectator box, he saw Drakonis, Isobel, Semaj, Mahogany, Dior, King Maj, Xinovioc and finally Cyarah. Chase turned to the other end of the arena where a gate was opening. He saw the announcer with a microphone in his hand standing at the edge of the arena.

"Creatures and Humans," the announcer yelled. "Welcome to the Crucible!" The people in the crowd started cheering, but Chase wasn't focused on them because there on the other side of the arena stood his opponent grinning like a madman.

The announcer yelled, "Let the first round begin!"

With a ring of the bell, Chase dashed towards the creature. He said "I am going to enjoy this..."

Made in the USA
San Bernardino, CA
26 July 2018